THE JUGGLER

JOHN MORRESSY

HENRY HOLT AND COMPANY
NEW YORK

THE JUGGLER

How unhappy is he who cannot forgive himself.

—PUBLILIUS SYRUS,
Moral Sayings

Henry Holt and Company, Inc.
Publishers since 1866
115 West 18th Street
New York, New York 10011

Henry Holt is a registered
trademark of Henry Holt and Company, Inc.

Published in Canada by Fitzhenry & Whiteside Ltd.,
195 Allstate Parkway, Markham, Ontario L3R 4T8.

Library of Congress Cataloging-in-Publication Data
Morressy, John. The juggler / John Morressy.
         p.   cm.
     Summary: Beran makes a pact with the devil to become
the greatest juggler in the world.
     [1. Juggling—Fiction.   2. Devil—Fiction.   3. Middle Ages—
Fiction.]   I. Title.   PZ7.M82714Ju   1996   [Fic]—dc20   95-33489

ISBN 0-8050-4217-2
First Edition—1996

Printed in the United States of America on acid-free paper.∞
10 9 8 7 6 5 4 3 2 1

To
EDWARD F. CARLSTROM
COLLEEN M. HEALY
GEOFFREY B. LISS
THOMAS F. KELLY
JOSEPH C. SCHIRO
and the staff of SARASOTA MEMORIAL HOSPITAL
and the HEART CENTER OF SARASOTA,

this book is dedicated with my profoundest gratitude. Without their prompt and expert help it would not have been written.

Contents

THE JUGGLER

The Benevolence of Count Osostro

The count Osostro enjoyed unlimited power in his domain, and he wielded his power with the caprice of a godling. He could spare a life with one breath and impose death with the next, dispense on one and the same occasion joy with his left hand and misery with his right. He could smile and be cruel; he could frown and be kind.

His deeds had become legend. It was said that on the same day he had in the morning taken up an aging widow found shivering at the gate of his palace, established her in his household, and ordered her marriage to one of his nobles, and that very afternoon had a beggar bludgeoned to death for crossing his path. The ways of the count Osostro were indeed unpredictable.

He loved diversions of every kind. He was fond of

novelty, and those who provided him with new delights were certain of a generous reward. Those who disappointed him were unfailingly punished in some ingenious way. His rewards were so extravagant that many were willing to risk his displeasure on the chance that they might enjoy his bounty. As the years passed, and the count found ever more unusual ways of expressing his dissatisfaction, the number of those who ventured to offer new amusements diminished, but never entirely ceased.

One year, in the drab and shrunken days before the onset of winter, the count was beset by boredom. He had enjoyed no new sport during the summer and fall, and he knew that he could look forward to fewer visitors, perhaps none at all, through the coming months of cold and snow. His mood grew ever darker. The court and the common people feared that the count might soon seek distraction in ways they would find disagreeable.

Then the juggler came. He had not been seen on the high road or in any of the outlying villages or settlements, nor had any of the guards at the outposts had any word of him. He simply appeared in the city one chilly day, took his place on a barrel head in a corner of the market square, and, without fanfare or announcement or any word at all, began to juggle.

He was a stranger of unprepossessing appearance

and uncertain age, tall and slender and hollow cheeked, with hair the color of old straw and a face lined by long exposure to wind and weather. His clothing was dusty and frayed, his boots cracked, his lean pack worn and patched. Yet he was someone new, and within minutes a crowd encircled him, and before long all other activity had ceased. Buyers and sellers alike forgot their mercantile interests and clustered around, jostling and pushing, to marvel at the astonishing feats of the juggler.

He began simply enough, with three daggers. Before long it was apparent that he was juggling more than three, but no one had seen him introduce another. Four, five, six daggers, perhaps more, were soon whirling and flashing above their heads. The juggler caught the eye of a child who stood at the edge of the crowd, entranced. At a nod from him she tossed him her doll, and immediately it was weaving its way among the blades. At his silent bidding, a young woman threw him a glove, and a man tossed him an empty mug. They, too, joined the shower of diverse objects.

All this time, though his lips moved silently, the juggler had said not a word. He did not, as some mountebanks and conjurers do, keep up a lively patter. He did not feign great effort or adopt a look of intense concentration. His brow was unfurrowed and his pale eyes were fixed before him. Save for a smile to the little girl, his expression had not varied. Indeed, he might almost have been described as having no expression at all. He seemed an onlooker to his own deeds, uninvolved and unimpressed, like a workman performing a difficult task for the thousandth time, out of sheer habit doing it with consummate grace and skill.

He stopped abruptly, catching the doll, the glove, and the mug in his hands while the daggers, seven of them, tattooed into the rim of the barrel head in a neat semicircle. The crowd burst into loud applause and cheering. A few tossed small coins to the makeshift platform and the adjacent ground. The juggler bowed, returned the items to their owners, and sprang lightly down to gather his reward. Several in the crowd called for more, but before the appeal spread, or the juggler could respond to it, the onlookers were thrust aside and a burly guardsman pushed his way through to confront the juggler.

"When did you enter the city?" the guardsman demanded.

"This very morning," said the juggler, rising from his knees.

"You will come with us to the palace and perform for our master, the count Osostro."

"As you wish," said the juggler. He took up his daggers, shouldered his meager pack, and, at the guardsman's back, set out for the palace.

That night, before Count Osostro, he repeated his

performance of the marketplace. The count was pleased. Two nights later, the juggler astonished everyone with the spectacle of little crystal spheres that seemed to appear in his hands from nowhere and flashed in a ring of brilliant ever-changing colors under the blaze of torches and candles, only to metamorphose one by one in midair into roses of varied colors. His third performance climaxed when the eggs he had been juggling, no bigger than the ball of his thumb, broke one by one and a tiny bird, singing sweetly, flew from each to circle the count's head and perch on the back of his throne.

Each time he performed, the juggler astounded his audience with some new and unexpected feat. But even the skills of a master could not delight for long a man of the count's demanding tastes. One evening, in the midst of the juggler's act, he grew bored and, on a whim, tossed a silver goblet to him. The juggler caught it without spilling a drop and managed to incorporate it into the rainbow of crystal vessels flashing above his head. The count, angered, seized another goblet and flung it, and then, very quickly, another. The juggler caught the second, but the third, thrown with the count's full force, struck him on the forehead and blinded him momentarily with the wine. He staggered; his rhythm broke, and a rain of vessels and goblets fell to the floor around him, the crystal shivering to bits, the goblets clattering and bouncing. Wine from the goblets soaked his tunic and spattered on the nearest guests.

The count laughed loudly in the sudden silence. "So, you're not so skilled after all," he said. He dismissed the juggler with a contemptuous "Away, charlatan," and a flick of his hand, and the juggler bowed and left the hall.

Next day he was nowhere to be found. When the count Osostro learned of the juggler's absence, he flew into a rage. The man had entered his domain without permission, and the count had overlooked the transgression. For him to dare to leave in the same manner was intolerable. The count Osostro did not permit anyone to presume upon his forbearance.

Guards were dispatched. The juggler was found on the high road, still within sight of the walls, and brought to the palace. He was taken before the count, and awaited judgment with an impassive expression.

"On the seven nights that you appeared before me, you entertained me. For that I will reward you. First with this purse of gold," said the count, tossing the juggler a purse the size of a large apple. The juggler took it up and dropped to one knee to acknowledge the count's generosity. The courtiers murmured in approbation and praise.

"I am not done," said the count. "As a further reward, I will allow you to choose which hand you are to lose as punishment for leaving my domain without permission."

The hall was still in an instant. The juggler blinked and paled slightly, but showed no other reaction. He extended his hands before him, looking from one to the other. After a pause he said, "It must be the count's own decision."

"If you refuse to make the choice, I will have your right hand."

The juggler closed his eyes and sighed. "Let it be so."

The count smoothed his short red beard thoughtfully and studied the man before him. "Then you are left-handed . . . or you wish me to think you are. Which is it?"

"I am not left-handed."

The count remained silent for a time; then he declared, "I have pronounced my judgment. Let his right hand be struck off." The guards took the juggler by either arm. No one else moved. The hall remained silent. The count turned to his chamberlain, who stood beside the seat of judgment, and said, "Do you think me too severe?"

The chamberlain was a decent man at heart, but he had learned to be circumspect in answering his master's questions. "Your Excellency's justice is beyond question. And yet . . . a lesser punishment might perhaps have served the purpose, and Your Excellency would be able to enjoy further displays of the man's skill."

The count laughed and shook his head. "Had I spared his hand, the fellow would still be able to perform for others. And since none is as capable of appreciating his skill or as generous in rewarding it as I, he would in time find himself before a less satisfactory audience. I have spared him a bitter disappointment."

The chamberlain bowed. "Your Excellency is judicious indeed."

"However, if anyone here feels that I have been unduly severe, then I will allow that gentle soul to offer his hand, or hers, in place of the juggler's," said the count. He scanned the hall slowly, a faint, expectant smile on his face. Few met his glance and no one spoke. His eyes came to rest on the juggler. "The others do not question my sentence. Do you?"

"No."

"Then my justice is manifest to all. Let it be done."

The sentence was carried out that very day. The count's physician attended, binding the stump of the severed hand and seeing that the juggler was cared for until he was fit to travel.

Next day, the count went hunting with his nobles. Though the hunt was successful, he returned to his palace in a dark mood and kept to himself for two full days, not emerging from his chamber in all that time.

He was heard to call out in the night, but he dismissed the guards who rushed to his aid.

At the end of five days, he visited the juggler, who was by now recovered from his ordeal. The physician, present on the count's order, was astonished to see the count take a small crystal jar from a pocket of his robe and hold it up.

"This ointment will ease the pain and assist in healing. I want it to be used, and used generously, for this man's relief," said the count, placing it in the physician's hand.

"But Your Excellency, this is the rarest of—" the physician began.

The count silenced him with "Do as I bid you." He drew forth a purse of gold larger than the first he had given the juggler, and laid it on the stones beside his victim's pallet.

"This is for you. You are free to leave whenever you choose. You are not a prisoner," the count told him.

"I will travel tomorrow, if it is your will," said the juggler.

"Let it be as you desire. You will have a horse, a fine gray gelding from my own stables."

The juggler looked at him in surprise, then knelt. "Your Excellency is most generous."

The count took him up and clapped him on the shoulder in a gesture of amity. "I have dispensed justice. It is my duty. Now I may show mercy. You understand that, do you not? What I did to you was just, was it not?"

"You have been just to me," said the juggler.

"Do you hear that, all of you?" said the count, turning first to the physician and then to the guards who stood by the door. "This man does not question my sentence." To the juggler he said, "Go then, and go in safety. You shall bear a letter that places you under my protection. No one will dare to raise a hand against you."

Before the juggler could express his thanks, the count turned and strode from the chamber. When the guards stepped to one side, the count stopped and motioned for them to walk ahead. As the men passed down the corridor, the physician saw the count glance back twice, quickly and nervously, as if he expected to see someone stealing up behind him.

The juggler left early the following morning. He wore new boots and a new outfit of fine cloth, gifts of the count Osostro. The gray gelding had been fitted out with a splendid saddle and harness. The saddlebags were filled with provisions, and a thick new blanket was rolled up behind. Tucked inside the juggler's tunic was a letter of safe passage bearing the count's own seal. He passed through the gate, onto the western road, and was never seen in the count's domain again.

1

The
Village

eran was the youngest of twelve children, six of whom were living. His oldest sisters were married to men of the village. His youngest sister, Joan, two years older than he, worked in the kitchen at Sir Morier's castle. Beran and his brother, Rolf, a year older than he, remained at home and worked the land with their parents.

His oldest brother had gone off to serve the king when Beran was still very small. He had returned once to visit them, and when the others were thought to be asleep, he had given his parents prizes he had taken during a campaign: a purse of gold and silver coins, and a gold ring with a red stone in it. Beran, lying awake, hoped to hear the story of the battle, but his brother said no more. The prizes were carefully hidden, and no one was to be told about them.

The village stood on a broad plateau just below the hilltop, the houses clustered together for safety. Everyone was near enough to hear his neighbor raise the hue and cry and come to his aid, and all could remove quickly to the castle in time of danger. The village held nearly two hundred people in its thirty-seven houses, each house with its garden plot in the adjoining croft. Beran's family had one of the best cottages in the village. It was thirty feet by sixteen, with solid corner posts, two windows, and two doors.

The villagers worked hard, and their work was well rewarded. The land was rich and fertile and the weather was clement. Harvests in recent years had been abundant. The animals were healthy and produced many young. Some of the old people talked of winters when entire families had starved or frozen to death in their homes, of rains that washed away a year's harvest in a single day, and of plagues that killed the pigs and cattle, but the younger ones had never seen such things. As far back as Beran could remember, there had always been food to eat, even in the winter. His family was especially fortunate, because Joan sometimes brought home scraps from the castle kitchen.

Sir Morier was a righteous man and a good protector. He dispensed justice fairly, if severely. He was generous in allowing his villagers firewood, and made no impossible demands on their labor, as some great ones were said to do. He often visited the villagers and talked with them, and Beran had seen him work at his father's side.

There was always talk of war, but the wars were something distant, fought in foreign lands for unfathomable reasons against men different from themselves. The villagers felt secure against the enemies of their king and lord, and from hunger and disease and the bands of lawless men who were said to roam the land. Life in the village was good, they said—certainly it was as good as any of them expected life on this earth to be—and they had much to be thankful for.

Beran was small of frame, but very quick and agile, with sharp eyes and deft hands. He had the patience and tenacity of a cat by a mouse hole. When something interested him, or puzzled him, he could sit for hours working on it until he had solved its mystery. Sir Morier himself had once called him "The Philosopher," and told the boy that he would send him to the university, where people did nothing but sit all day and think about things, but Beran knew that this was all a joke. The university was as remote from his life as were the stars. He would live out his life in the village, marry the woman chosen for him, raise his family and work for as long as he was able, grow old and die, and be buried in the little plot where his brothers and sisters lay. He was neither happy nor unhappy at the prospect; it was the way things would be, and he accepted it without question. One might as well question the rising and setting of the sun.

One day he went to the market town with his father and about a score of men from the village to attend a fair. They took a well-marked trail through the wood and were wary every step of the way. All the men wore daggers at their belts. Some carried cudgels. It was Beran's first time away from the village. He was a little frightened, but when at last they came to the fair and he saw the people, more people than he had ever seen in his life, and all of them busy and noisy and bustling about, his fear gave way to excitement. His father appointed a meeting place, then went about his business and left Beran to his own devices. The boy wandered wide-eyed through the crowds, drinking in the unfamiliar sights and sounds.

He quickly accustomed himself to the stir and the color, the shouting and calling back and forth, the strange people and the animals and the loud laughter. Except for greater numbers and the odd dress of some, the fair was not, after all, so very different from his village on a feast day. There was really only one great difference, and he soon discovered it: A company of traveling players had set up a couple of planks for a platform, with a brightly painted cloth as backdrop, and were performing. Beran squeezed his way through the crowd up to the very front, where he watched in fascination. He had never seen anything like this in his life, never heard of such things, never dreamed that such people existed.

A man in colorful clothing bent over backward, farther and farther, until it seemed he must fall down, but instead of falling, he kept on bending until he was able to thrust his head out between his knees and make faces at the crowd, all the while saying things to make them laugh. He then planted his elbows on the platform, took up a drum, and, balancing it atop his head, began to beat out a rhythm with his feet while he rested on his forearms, his chin cupped in his hands. A woman in a long dress covered with ribbons did a slow dance to the drumbeat. She made colored scarfs flutter about her in curling patterns. When the dance was done, she flung up her hands and the scarfs all vanished at once. Beran cried out in astonishment, but she was not done. She plucked a bright red scarf out of the air, rolled it up, and put it in her mouth, and then breathed out flame. She did this several times, sending a stream of fire farther than the reach of her outstretched fingertips. When she was done making fire, she drew all the scarfs from her mouth, one by one, unscorched and as bright as ever. After that, she did other tricks, making things disappear and then reappear in unexpected places, taking a coin out of one man's ear and a squawking hen from another's hood. Beran was beside himself with amazement and delight.

The man then came forward, threw three brightly colored balls into the air, and began to juggle them, arcing them back and forth between his hands. The woman threw him a fourth ball, and he worked it into the pattern, and then she threw a fifth. By now the balls were a colored blur. The man sank down to a kneeling position, then seated himself on a little stool that the woman had moved into place behind him. He climbed onto the stool and tilted it until it was balanced on one leg. He then balanced himself on one foot atop the stool. Finally, he sprang off to his feet again, all the time without dropping a ball.

Beran watched the steady shuttling motion of his hands, studying every move, unable to take his eyes away. He had never seen a man juggle before, and it impressed him more than all the other feats. When the man caught the five balls in his hands and gave a loud laugh, and the crowd cried out their approval, Beran could not contain himself. He sprang up and shouted, "I want to do that!"

The crowd all laughed, and the juggler dropped to one knee, looked down on the boy, and said, "So you want to be a juggler, do you?"

Beran had never heard the word before. He could only say, "I want to do what you do!"

The man and the woman laughed, and the crowd laughed along with them. Someone took Beran under the arms and swung him up to the platform. He did not understand what was funny, but he laughed along with the rest.

"How much can you pay for lessons?" the man asked.

"He looks like a rich one. I bet he has plenty," the woman said, and the crowd laughed some more.

"I have a piece of bread," Beran said.

The juggler staggered back, as if astonished. "I've found a wealthy patron! I'll buy a palace and fill it with servants! I'll never work again!" he said, reeling drunkenly about the platform.

"First you'll buy me fine clothes and jewels," the woman said, strutting about the stage in an imitation of a grand lady displaying her finery.

"Will you show me?" Beran asked.

"Teach him to juggle!" someone called out from the crowd. Others took up the cry. The man raised his hands to silence them, and announced, "Only because I have been offered such a generous reward, such a lavish gift, will I reveal to this lad the secret of my art. But first, may I have the bread?" he said, turning to Beran and bowing deeply.

Beran took the scrap of bread from his scrip. The man lifted it high, turned it over, examined it back and front, sniffed it, made a face, and as the crowd laughed louder and louder, he pretended to bite into it, then roared and held his jaw as if he had broken it. Maneuvering his jaw from side to side, he said,

"How long have you been carrying that bread around, boy?"

"Only since this morning."

The man turned to the crowd with an expression of disbelief; then he took a real bite and chewed slowly, making faces all the time, until he had finished the bread. Then he rubbed his hands together briskly and said, "Now I will teach this boy to juggle. Let the lessons begin!"

He tossed a brightly colored ball to Beran. It was surprisingly light. "Throw it up in the air and catch it with the other hand," he said. Beran did so, and the juggler turned to the crowd and said, "Behold, a natural talent! He juggles one ball with the skill of a master!" He threw Beran a second ball and said, "Toss them from hand to hand, one after the other." Beran again did as the man bid, and the crowd shouted and cheered. "A prodigy!" the juggler cried. "A wonder! Now, if he can do as well with three as he can with two . . ." He tossed a third ball. With a ball in each hand, Beran tried to catch the third, but missed it and dropped one of the others. The man picked it up and handed it to him, then stood with his hands on his hips, looking at him impatiently. "Well, go ahead. Juggle. Don't you want to learn to juggle?" he said.

Beran threw all three balls into the air and caught one. The others went rolling about the platform. He chased them and gathered them up. He tried again, throwing one, and then another, but dropping both when he tossed up the third. The crowd was laughing now, and calling out to him.

"Keep them in the air, boy, not on the ground!" someone in the crowd shouted, and other voices followed.

"He's no juggler!"

"Show us the real thing!"

The juggler shrugged his shoulders. Bending low, he said softly, "You heard the people, boy. They've seen all they want of you."

"Won't you teach me?"

"You've had all the lessons you can buy for a piece of bread. If you want me to teach you, bring me silver."

The woman quickly added, "For both of us. A silver stater each, and we'll teach you everything we know."

"I don't have silver."

"Then you'll grow oats and barley all your life, boy. Away with you now." The juggler lifted him by the waist and swung him high, then let him down lightly at the front of the crowd.

Beran said nothing of this adventure to his father. When they were home again, he told his brother everything. Rolf, still angry that Beran and not he had gone to the market, said that Beran had been foolish. Rolf had once heard tell of a juggler—the very same one, he believed—and he told Beran that a boy like him could never learn to do such things.

"Why not?"

"Those people are different from us. They're in league with the devil, I've heard."

Beran thought for a time. "Maybe the woman was, but not the juggler. He didn't do anything magical. I could learn to do it."

"You can't learn those things all by yourself."

"Yes, I can. I watched him. I know what he did."

Rolf made a contemptuous gesture of dismissal. "Then go ahead and learn. And what good will it do you here in the village? There's work to be done. You have no time for tricks."

"I won't stay in the village."

"You can't leave. You'll never get permission."

"Our brother left."

"The king needed him. Sir Morier didn't like to let him go. He wants us to stay here, where we belong."

"I'll leave without his permission, then."

Rolf sprang at Beran, knocking him over backward. He struck him hard across the face and held him down. He said, "Don't ever talk like that. If you ran away, we'd all be in trouble."

"I'd come back in a year or two. I'd have a purse full of gold."

"You're stupid. Don't talk that way," Rolf said.

The next day Beran made three soft balls from old rags. From then on, whenever he had a spare moment, he worked at juggling. He had watched the juggler's hands very closely, and he remembered the way they moved. He tried again and again to match the fluid motion, but it was easier to picture it in his mind than to duplicate it with his hands. On the first few attempts the balls collided in midair, but he finally learned to toss one slightly under the other. He practiced with a single ball first, accustoming his hands to the motion, and then he tried two. Learning to handle the third one was difficult. Sometimes he managed to get all three going and catch them, but then he could not repeat the motion without dropping one, or two, or all three, and sometimes when this happened he felt that he would never learn. But he persisted, and finally, after many days of frustration, he was able to keep three balls in the air.

He practiced every day in secret. As he improved, he took less care to keep his skills hidden. When he was sure of himself, he demonstrated his newfound ability to Rolf. His brother was surprised by Beran's skill, but he had no praise for him.

"Why do you want to do that?" Rolf said. "It will only cause trouble."

"How can juggling cause trouble?"

"You'll try to leave the village. You said so."

"No, I won't. I'll stay right here."

"And what good is juggling here in the village?"

"When I get really good, I'll go to Sir Morier and show him what I can do. He'll want me to live at the castle, and juggle for him and his friends and visitors."

"If you go to Sir Morier with your tricks, he'll have you beaten for your idleness."

Beran said nothing more. Rolf was always like this, always cautious and worried about anything that was not just the way things had always been. He wanted to stay here in the village for the rest of his life and live as his parents and neighbors did, and their parents before them.

Beran had never thought much about the future before, but now that he had learned this new skill, he thought that he might do something different from everyone else. He had put aside his thoughts of leaving the village. Rolf was right about that. Sir Morier would never grant him permission, and the penalty for leaving without it would fall heavily on his family. Besides, the world beyond the village, though it held interesting sights and strange people, was full of dangers both known and unknown. It would be good to live at the castle and perform for Sir Morier and other great folk.

Beran did not shirk his duties. When he was not working, he practiced. It was difficult at first, but he improved with time. By the next spring he could juggle four balls. He had carved them for himself out of light wood, dyeing them in bright colors like the ones used by the man at the market.

His skill became known throughout the village. His parents at first disapproved, but when they found that others admired him, they relented. In the fields, the others called upon him to juggle for them while they ate and rested. In return, they did a share of his work. Beran was pleased with the way things were working out. He felt that Sir Morier, once he returned for the winter, would surely take notice of him, and then he would be called to the castle.

One autumn day, toward the end of the harvest, Beran was working in the outermost field. He left the others to fetch water from a spring at the top of a nearby hill. The afternoon was sultry, and even on the heights the air was almost still. The climb tired him, and when he reached the top, he crept into the shade of a low thicket to rest for a time. He went to sleep almost at once.

He awoke at the sound of horses' hooves. They were moving slowly and cautiously over the bare rock of the hilltop. He lay unmoving, listening closely. There were many horses, and they were all around him.

He heard voices, and his heart almost stopped when he realized that they were speaking in a tongue he had never heard before. They were strangers, and the coming of strangers always meant trouble for the village. He tried to look out, but the thicket was too dense. He could only listen. He heard the jingling of harness, the splash of water, men speaking, and some laughter. It was hard, cold laughter with no trace of humor in it. Then the hoofbeats, still slow and stealthy, moved off on all sides.

When some time had passed without any sound of the intruders, he crawled from the thicket. No one was to be seen, but there were hoofprints everywhere and the ground all around the spring was churned up. Keeping low, Beran looked down the hillside to see where the horsemen had gone. They were spreading out along the line of trees, and as he watched, they disappeared into the greenery.

Beran did not know what to do. Sir Morier had been summoned away and taken many of his men with him. Only a small force remained at the castle. His first thought was to shout a warning, but the fields were far away and the slight breeze was against him; his voice would not carry. He had to signal somehow. The treetops obscured him from the outermost fields, where the horsemen would strike first, but he could just be seen in the village. In desperation, he took off his shirt and waved it over his head, but he saw no sign of recognition. Even if his signal had been seen, who could know that it was a warning of danger?

He sank down on the bare stone, trembling with fear and frustration. When he looked up, he saw a thin column of smoke rising from just beyond the trees. Soon a second and third column joined the first, and then others, until all joined in a single pall. The breeze

carried faint shouts and cries to him. Beyond the treetops, the horsemen emerged into view, tiny but dis-
tinct, riding toward the castle. Soon flames and smoke
were rising from the castle.

Beran did not dare to stay near the spring, for fear
that the horsemen would return the way they had
come, or others might come to join them. He dared not
go near the village. He spent the night in the ravine,
huddled in the shelter of two fallen trees. In the morning the fields and the castle were still smoking. He
waited until midday, and when he saw no horsemen
and no signs of life, he ventured into the village.

It lay in ruins. The main way had been churned into
a mire of mud, blood, and ashes. Bodies lay in the
narrow lanes, or huddled in groups where they had
been herded together for easy slaughter. All the live-
stock was gone. Except for the sucking sound of his
feet in the muck, the silence was complete. Even the
birds were gone from this scene of desolation.

Like most of the others, his home had been put to
the torch. Two walls were completely gone and the
roof had burned away. Beran's parents and brother lay
together in a corner, covered in dried blood. Both his
parents had been stabbed many times. Rolf had an axe
in his hands. His head had been crushed and misshapen by a tremendous blow.

Everything in the cottage had been destroyed. The
boards and trestles of the table, the two stools, the

barrel and buckets, had all been smashed, the handles of the tools broken, the yoke hacked and splintered. The beds had been slashed open and the dried husks scattered over the floor.

It was the same everywhere, destruction and death, all in a few minutes of an autumn afternoon. Beran wandered to the edge of the village, and there he sat and wept. Who had done this? Why? The village had no enemies. It was at war with no one. The outlaw bands who raided from time to time came to steal, not to kill and destroy. These horsemen came from somewhere else, a place where men spoke a different tongue. What had brought their wrath upon this village?

After a time, hunger made him rise. He had not eaten since the previous midday, and now that the first shock was past, he felt the full bite of the emptiness in his stomach. He searched the village, but found nothing. What had not been carried off had been spilled or burned.

He trudged up the hill to the castle. He was in the open now, plainly visible to any watcher, but he did not think of the danger. He had seen no living soul since coming to the village, and expected to see none.

Sir Morier's home was only a larger and more strongly made version of the surrounding cottages, but the villagers all thought of it, and spoke of it, as the castle. He was their overlord; his home, with its thick walls and heavy oaken door, was their stronghold and their refuge. Now it was as silent as the village. All the outlying buildings had been burned, and smoke still rose from the granary and stables. The castle doors were splintered and broken. Here the invaders had met their only real resistance.

Beran saw the bodies of tall, pale-skinned men with fair hair. All but one had short beards, some of a reddish-bronze, some of gold, and some so fair that they were almost white, although the men were young. Near them were two fallen attackers dark in coloring, short and muscular, with thick black hair and skin the color of dry earth. All the invaders carried the same kind of weapons as the men of the castle, but their shields were made of wood and leather. They must have been good fighters, Beran thought, for around many of their fallen lay two or three of Sir Morier's men.

The fighting had been fiercest at the keep. The fallen here were piled one atop another, and pairs of men lay locked in a death grip. Beran had to climb over bodies to enter the hall.

Here, instead of destruction, there had been looting. All the plates and drinking vessels were gone. The silver cross and candlesticks and the gold chalice were missing from the chapel, and the gold-and-silver door of the tabernacle had been torn off. Vestments lay strewn about the floor, where they had been flung in the search for plunder. The chaplain was sprawled at the foot of the altar, his head and arm almost severed, the blood from a dozen wounds darkening his vestments.

Beran found his sister and the other household workers in the kitchen, every one of them dead. The kitchen and cellars were stripped. Part of a small ham and a loaf of bread had been dropped, and a few turnips. He sat down to eat then and there, on the kitchen floor. When he was done, he drank a few mouthfuls of ale that still remained in a shattered cask.

Having eaten, he took stock of his situation. He was the only one left. For the first time in his life, he had no one to tell him what to do. He had no parents. He had no older brother or sister, and no master. He could do as he pleased and go where he wished, asking no one's permission. It was a frightening thought, but an exciting one.

He bundled the rest of the ham and bread in a cloth from the kitchen, and started out of the keep. As he passed a pile of bodies, he saw that one of the attackers had a purse in his fist; he must have been struck down in the very act of looting. Beran hesitated for a moment, then snatched the purse from the stiff fingers. It held two gold pieces and a large quantity of silver, along with some smaller coins. He thought then of the prize his brother had left with their parents. It was no use to them now, and it might help him to stay alive.

As he left the hall, he had a terrible fright. One of the fallen attackers in the tangle of bodies by the door groaned and raised his head. The man's face and chest were covered in blood from a gaping wound in his forehead, but somehow he had survived. Beran froze where he stood. The man groaned again, a sound of terrible pain. He dragged himself to his feet and took a single step forward. He did not seem to see Beran, though his eyes were open. He said something in his strange tongue and struck out with one arm as if battling an enemy; then he pitched forward and lay still.

The man was alive. Beran could hear his breath coming in great gasps. He looked down and remembered his parents and his sister and Rolf, all so cruelly stabbed and battered. His fear gave way to hatred and a desire for vengeance. Perhaps this was the very man who had slain them; if not, he was part of the murderous, thieving crew, as guilty as the one who had done the deed.

Moving quietly, Beran put down his bundle and took up a sword from one of the fallen. It was so heavy he could barely lift it. He poised it over the fallen raider and with all his strength drove it into the man's back, just below the shoulder blade. It grated against bone, stuck for just an instant, then slid deep into his trunk. He groaned once more, not very loudly, let out a long sigh, and then his breathing stopped.

Beran drew back from the body, his hatred purged in

an instant. All he wanted now was to get away. He imagined other fallen invaders rising up and lunging toward him, and he took a dagger from one of the bodies for protection. Beran snatched up his bundle and ran. He reached his parents' cottage without another incident, and dug his brother's prizes from the spot by the corner post where his father had buried them.

The invaders had come from west of the village. He set out toward the east. He had no destination. He wanted only to be elsewhere, and never to return to this place again.

2

The
Road

The forest surrounding the village was a menacing wilderness where men traveled in armed groups and kept to the marked paths. Beran had heard tales of its perils ever since he was a child. Beasts and savage men lurked in its depths. False trails turned and circled upon themselves, leading nowhere. A lone wanderer might be robbed or murdered if he kept to the main track. Once away from it, he would lose his way and starve or freeze to death, if he did not first fall victim to wild creatures or to something worse. Things neither human nor animal roamed the forest, and against them there was no defense but the help of heaven.

The village had always meant home, refuge, the place of family and friends and safety. That was so no longer. The forest was danger. Home and refuge, family and friends, the village and the people he had known, all had been destroyed in one terrible day. He could not remain in the village, amid corpses and ashes. The wolves and carrion eaters would quickly learn of the waiting feast, and a helpless boy would be as welcome a morsel as the dead. Sir Morier might not return for a long time, perhaps not at all. Beran had no choice. His world was now the world that lay beyond, and to reach it he must brave the forest alone.

He wandered in its depths for days, living off berries and nuts and fish from the brooks when his small store was gone. At first his heart jumped at every noise. He started awake in terror a hundred times on his first night. But by the end of the third day his fear had diminished. The noises did him no harm, and he saw nothing but small, harmless creatures scurrying out of his way, as afraid of him as he had been of unseen sounds. He awoke every morning cold and stiff and hungry, but the sun soon warmed him, and he always found something to eat, though never enough to satisfy the emptiness that growled and gnawed like a trapped beast in his belly.

After eight days he came to the edge of the forest. Before him, beyond the cleared ground, was the road. Here the world began.

He watched as a pair of riders went westward at a brisk gallop, and not long after, a small band of men and women passed to the east on foot. For a long time he saw no one, and then a cart heaped with corn came into view moving slowly from the west. A tall, bearded man bearing a staff led the single horse. He went watchfully, continuously glancing from one side of the road to the other.

Beran swallowed his fear and raced from the forest. As he neared the wagon, the man turned and they caught sight of each other.

"Bread! Please, master, a bit of bread!" Beran cried.

The man raised his staff to bar closer approach. Beran stopped and sank to his hands and knees, panting.

"Who are you, boy? Where do you come from?" the man called to him.

"I've been lost in the forest. Please, master, I'm hungry!"

"Where's your village?"

"Back there," Beran said, gesturing to the forest. "It's gone. Raiders came. Everyone's dead."

The man shaded his eyes with one hand and surveyed the clearing on both sides. After a careful study, he beckoned to Beran and said, "Come on, boy. I can spare you a bit of food. Hurry along, we must keep moving."

The man, whose name was Alan, provided Beran with a thick slice of bread and a slab of cheese, and gave him ale from a jug. As they went on, he heard the boy's story, shaking his head often and muttering, "Terrible, terrible," very softly, but he said nothing more.

Beran traveled with Alan for two days, helping wherever he could, though there was little for him to do but walk behind the wagon and see that nothing was lost. Alan remained silent most of the time, never smiling. He responded to Beran's questions and observations with a word or two. On the second evening, without preamble of any kind, Alan said, "I know some people who lost a son last year. They could use a good lad to help them."

Beran was excited at first and shouted his gratitude aloud. Here was a chance to be part of a village again, to have a home, a family, and a master. No longer would he wander alone, like a wolf; he would have a fixed place in the world. For a time he could think of nothing else and was eager to meet these people and take up his new life.

That evening, when they had eaten, he decided to repay Alan's generosity in the only way he could, by juggling for him. But no sooner had he begun than the man slapped the wooden balls aside and seized his arm roughly. He said, "What's this foolishness, boy? Throw away those wicked toys. There's no place for clowns and jugglers among honest people."

Beran pulled free and picked up the balls that lay in the dust. He was hurt and confused by the rebuke. "The people in my old village liked it," he said. "They'd do my work for me if I juggled for them."

"Then they were as silly as you are. There'll be no

one in your new village to do your work while you play."

As he lay under the wagon that night, Beran thought of life in his new village. It sounded like a joyless place. To be alone in the forest was bad, and to go hungry was most unpleasant. But to spend the rest of his life working among people who would not allow him to do what he did well and wanted to do better and better—this was a dismal prospect.

He thought and thought, drifted off to sleep and woke again to think some more, and at last made his decision. It was good to be safe, but one could pay too high a price for safety. Before dawn, while Alan was still snoring regularly, Beran rose and slipped away.

From that day he was a wayfarer. Days became months, and the months passed into years, and still he traveled without family, home, or friends, sometimes with a companion but more often alone, through a world where danger was everywhere and kindness and compassion were as rare as a midsummer frost.

The life of the road was different from anything he had known before. In the village, everyone was much alike, although he had not noticed it as clearly as he now did. The villagers had had their different ways, but they had all dressed alike, used the same phrases, complained of the same problems, voiced the same hopes. The people he saw and met on the road were of all kinds.

There were laborers who had broken their bond and fled their village, and fugitives from the king's justice. Such men were dangerous, and he avoided them. There were messengers, riding in great haste on worldly business, stopping for no one, riding down any who blocked their path. There were peddlers and beggars, cobblers and tinkers and healers and honest workingmen, musicians and bearwards and animal keepers. Some of them were kindly men, full of jokes and songs and stories, and willing to share their scanty store with him in return for a few simple feats of juggling, and sometimes out of pure kindness. But many were hard and cruel, and drove him off with a threat and a blow, or set a dog on him.

There were pilgrims, some of them penitents in chains and fetters making their slow and painful way to distant holy places to atone for wrongs they had done, some of them journeying to fulfill a promise made in time of need or illness, or to give thanks for heaven-sent aid. Some, rich and mighty, traveled in great state, with a baggage train of food and wines and fine plate and rich garments following for their ease and convenience. And some who bore the scrip and staff were actually discontented laborers seeking new opportunity, ready to throw aside their pilgrim trappings and take up their tools again when safely beyond their rightful lord's reach.

There were the king's men, and the great lords, and

they were best given a wide berth. They traveled in large companies, with archers and men-at-arms preceding them to make their way secure, many horsemen, and wagons laden with food and wine and heaped documents of state. In some of the wagons were ladies of the court. They did not want commoners near them, and the commoners were kept far off.

There were the beggars who feigned leprosy or blindness or covered their bodies with hideous false sores, or dragged themselves along the ground as cripples, crying out for alms. Some others pretended to be maddened by spirits, or driven into fits. A few of these frauds were clever and good-natured, and generous to a hungry boy.

And there were criminals of every kind. The ones he feared most were those who simply killed and robbed when the opportunity presented itself, squandered the loot at inn and brothel, and set out to look for the next victim. He knew that such men would welcome him like an old friend, joke with him, and kill him for the price of the rags on his back.

The first winter was the hardest time, and more than once Beran was certain he would freeze to death. He always managed to find some kind of shelter, but for months on end, he was never warm. Even with coins in his purse, there were many times when he could not purchase food, and times when he dared not.

Out of necessity he learned to steal. His hands were quick and deft, and he was fast of foot, so he had success. He stole seldom, only in dire need, and always worked alone. He was always cautious. The punishment for theft was summary and severe.

He practiced juggling at every opportunity. Sometimes he entertained others at a roadside resting place, or at an inn, and they praised his skill and gave him a place by the fire and a share of their food. But even when he was being praised and rewarded, he knew that his tricks were simple and he had much to learn about juggling.

He had other things to learn, as well. He quickly learned that a person could smile and speak fair words and act cruelly. One early lesson nearly cost him his life. He found that it was dangerous, and might be fatal, for a small boy with no protector to show a silver coin. Even a grown man, well armed and among friends, was a fool to boast of a full purse.

After that first narrow escape, Beran kept his small hoard concealed, but the memory preyed on his mind. He began to suspect that every stranger he encountered knew of his wealth and was determined to take it from him. He was slight and wiry and not very strong; his only defense was flight. He was uneasy by day, when he was plainly visible to everyone, and anxious by night, when every shadow might conceal an enemy. His sleep was fitful. He was reluctant to go among strangers, yet aware of the perils of traveling alone. The little purse of coins and the ring weighed upon him like shackles. He was loath to cache them away, but knew no one to whom he could entrust them.

He finally resolved his problem at one impulsive stroke. He had been given shelter for the night in the guest house of a monastery and treated with kindness by an aged monk. After a simple supper, before he lay down to sleep, he asked to speak with the prior, saying that he had a gift. He laid his treasure before the prior, a thin, pale man with one clouded eye. The prior fixed his good eye on Beran and scrutinized him closely. Beran appeared an unlikely benefactor. Ragged and dirty, a boy traveling alone, he was far more likely to be a thief disposing of his plunder before he could be caught.

Beran told a story close to the truth: He explained that the gold and silver were his brother's, won in the service of the king, and the ring was the gift of a great lord for bravery in battle. His brother had solemnly instructed him, should anything befall their parents, to give all to the monks so that prayers and masses might be said for their souls. The prior questioned him on several details. When he was satisfied by the boy's story, he accepted the gift gratefully.

"You have done a holy and a blessed thing. Your brother is a loving son, and so are you," said the prior. "How did your parents die?"

"Our village was raided. They were slain."

"And what is to become of you? Is there no one to take you in?"

"Everyone in the village is dead."

"You are young to be alone. We might find a place for you here."

Beran had no wish to stay with the monks. They were kindly men, but their way of life was too austere for his liking. He preferred the road. Dangerous though it might be, it was never dull.

By this time he had learned to lie convincingly. "You are generous, Father, but I must go to my brother, in the Holy Land."

"A long and perilous journey for one so young. But it is a blessed undertaking. May God be with you."

"Thank you, Father."

The prior did not speak for a time, and Beran waited patiently for his dismissal. But then the prior said abruptly, as if he had come to a decision, "A company of pilgrims leave us in the morning. They are not bound for the Holy Land, but you can travel south with them until your ways part, and then join another band. I will ask them to take you. You would be safer among them."

Pilgrims could be even stricter in their behavior than the monks, but Beran saw no point in refusing the offer. This group might turn out to be good companions, well supplied with food. In any event, he could travel in their company until he found better.

He left the next morning with eight pilgrims on their way to the shrine of Saint James at Compostela. The pilgrims went on foot, each man carrying a staff, with a leather scrip tied at his waist. All wore the simple tunic of the pilgrim, marked with the cross. Even though the air was cold enough to show their breath and patches of snow still lay in shaded places off the road, three of them walked barefoot.

Their leader was a tall, broad-shouldered man with grizzled hair and a pale scar down one cheek. His name was Julian, and he was a knight. He was the most talkative one of the group. At the prior's urging, he had taken Beran in charge, and before they had passed out of sight of the monastery, he and the boy were talking freely. Beran gave a fairly accurate version of his story, and Julian responded by telling something of himself.

"I was steeped in the ways of the world and its deceits," he told Beran as they walked. "War and hunting and revelry and violence, greed and pride and worse things were my pleasures. For the poor and the sick I cared nothing. I lived as I pleased, and gave no thought to what must await me after such a life. I have seen scores of men—nay, hundreds—die suddenly, with no time to prepare themselves, and yet I paid no heed to the warnings God was sending me through them. Like so many others, I told myself that I would win over God and the saints by gifts of land and gold when my hour came. Fool! I never gave a thought to good works and penitence."

Beran had traveled with pilgrims before, and knew their way of talking. It seemed to him that the holier a man was, the worse things he said of himself, while the truly wicked men blamed themselves for nothing. But he did not say this to Julian. He saw the scarred hands and missing finger, the pale rosette of an arrow wound in the forearm, and he believed Julian's words about a life of violence. This was a man who had seen death, and dealt it out.

"One night I had a terrible dream," the knight went on. "I found myself in a place of flames and torment. A voice cried out to me, 'This punishment awaits you, Julian, unless you turn from your evil ways, and repent, and make atonement. Turn, and pray for yourself and for me.' I recognized the voice at once. It was my old companion James, who had died at my side in battle against the pagans in Prussia. James was a far better man than I, yet he was suffering for his sins. How much greater would my suffering be!" Julian was silent for a time, and from the look on his hard face, Beran could tell that he was thinking of that visionary dream. Turning to the boy, his expression earnest, he said, "I arose at once and began to make preparations. The message was clear. For both our sakes I must go to the shrine of Saint James. I wrote my will, and went to all whom I had offended, to make peace with them. Then I went to the church to confess my sins and be invested as a pilgrim."

"Did you have to do all those things before you could begin?" Beran asked, for though he had spoken with scores of pilgrims, many of their ways remained mysterious to him.

"Without a sincere confession, and atonement for past wrongs, the pilgrimage would be a mockery. I have heard of pilgrims who were struck down at the very shrine, and others who were unable to pass through the church doors, because they had not prepared themselves."

Beran was deeply impressed to hear this. Even more impressive was the explanation he received from another of the pilgrims, an aged man named William, of the significance of the items in the pilgrim's outfit, a uniform as distinctive as a priest's robes or a knight's armor. Every item stood as a symbol of something invisible and unseen, and Beran listened with awe and growing confusion as William, in a soft, unhurried voice barely more than a whisper, told how the burdon, the sturdy metal-footed staff of the pilgrim, was not merely an aid to walking and a means of defense; its wood symbolized the tree that had caused the downfall of mankind and the cross that had purchased redemption. As the cross was our defense against the devil, so the staff defended the pilgrim against wild dogs and wolves and others who would assail him as the devil assails the soul. The staff serves as a third leg for the pilgrim, recalling the three persons of the Trinity. As the pilgrim leans on the bourdonnée, or the staff, so the bourdonnée also symbolizes faith, while the scrip, a bag too small to hold more than a few coins and scraps of food, reminds the pilgrim of holy poverty and of his duty of charity and almsgiving. The tunic, by its rough cloth, recalls the humanity of Christ, while the cross sewn upon it attests to His divinity.

Beran was able to follow William's words thus far. But when the old man began to expound on deeper matters, and draw out significations of such subtlety that each was more astounding than the one before, the boy lost his way and sat mystified, stunned by the thought that things so commonplace and plain to the eye could be wrapped in such layers of solemn meaning.

William could speak simply and clearly when the occasion required. One day they were forced off the road by a party of horsemen trailing a long caravan of wagons. The horsemen, richly dressed and attended by an army of servants, offered no greeting, did not pause or even glance at the pilgrims, but rode on, with their goods following behind in wagons.

"Such are the worldly," William said to Beran as they looked on. "They travel in luxury and call it penance. But those who enjoy their paradise in this world will pay dearly in the next."

Luxury was a word of vague meaning to Beran. He had heard people speak as though it consisted of silken tents, golden dishes heaped with food, the certainty of warmth and shelter and safety, and if this were so, then luxury seemed to him to be a very good thing indeed. He had known comfort a few times in his life, when he sat by a fire with his belly full and no one threatening or abusing him. He imagined luxury to be like that, only much better. It would mean never being hungry or cold or wet or afraid; it would mean being heeded and obeyed. He wondered why William disliked it so, but did not ask.

William and Julian were the boy's chosen companions on the journey, the old man for his serene wisdom, the knight for the chance that he might tell something of his past life, which was sure to be exciting. Beran divided his time between them, never intruding on their private thoughts or conversations but always remaining near one or the other. But Julian, having once told his story, had put his past behind him, and William was in poor health, stopping often to rest and growing too weak to spend breath on needless talk.

On Beran's fourth day of traveling with them, William collapsed and could not rise. The pilgrims reached a monastery that night, Julian bearing the frail old man on his back as if he were a child, and William was taken at once to the infirmary. He died surrounded by his companions, who prayed and sang. They remained to bury him and pray for his soul. Beran left the next morning with a large company of pilgrims bound for Vézelay.

Two days among them was more than enough for him. These people did not talk, they only walked, at a relentless pace, and prayed constantly. They carried no food, depending entirely on the charity of those they encountered. When he saw the bush of an ale house at the roadside, Beran marked the place, and toward evening he slipped away from the pilgrims to return to it.

Outside the doorway, under a tree, two men lay on the ground, very drunk, singing loudly and incoherently. Beran almost fell over one of them, but the man seemed not to notice. Within, the ale house was a noisy, lively place, full of men and women of all sorts laughing and talking and calling to one another. Beran saw more than a score of people, most of them seated on benches around a table. Some were in rags; others, by their dress, were tradesmen. A few, Beran suspected, were outlaws. They were a merry crowd, busily enjoying themselves, and they paid no heed to a boy all alone.

In his wanderings Beran had learned the shifts and devices that serve those who can depend on neither strength nor wealth nor powerful friends, the age-old ways of those who survive by their own cunning. He stooped over, dropped one shoulder, and bent one arm and hand into an awkward position, like a cripple. Limping to the longest table, he began to juggle two balls with the other hand, keeping it up until he had caught the attention of the revelers.

"See what a poor feeble boy can do, my masters and ladies!" he said in a weak, pained voice. "I am all sunken and shrunken with hunger and thirst. Now, if I were given a bit to eat, and something good to drink, I might be able to entertain you with astonishing feats."

"Away with the beggar!" said a fat man at the far end of the table, but a woman quickly broke in, "Let's see his tricks. Give the boy a bit of meat, Gib, and let's see what he can do."

The man at her side tore a wing from the fowl before him and flung it to Beran. The boy snatched up the meat and gobbled it down greedily. A man next to him pushed his tankard forward, and Beran took a deep draft of ale. Wiping his greasy hand on his thigh, he said, "Masters, your kindness has healed me!" Flexing his other hand dramatically, he straightened up and began to juggle three balls, meanwhile skipping about in an improvised dance. The drinkers at the table laughed and cheered him on. After a minute of this, he stopped, wiped his brow, and said, "Now, if I had a belly full of good food, I could do wondrous things."

A pale, dark-haired man in plain dark clothing tossed him a couple of pennies. "Here, boy, fill your belly, but first let us see your best." At the woman's urging, the man who had given him the meat now gave him a penny, and two others added a similar contribution.

"Thank you, kind lady, and you, masters all," Beran said, bowing and drawing in the coins. "I feel much stronger." He started with the three balls, and one by one he added flourishes to his performance. He tossed a ball under his leg, then tossed and caught balls behind his back. By this time, others had gathered around the table, and they were cheering him on. He paused, then held up four balls and began to juggle with them. Suddenly, for no apparent reason, the fat man rose from his place, red-faced, and shouted at him, shaking his fist and taking up a tankard as if to throw it. A man next to the fat man seized his arm, and another jumped on the two of them—whether to make peace or to provoke a fight it was impossible to tell—and in an instant the three were on the floor and the crowd's attention was on them.

Beran cared little about the outcome. He put away the four balls and looked for a quiet corner where he might enjoy a meal. He felt a grip on his arm, and turning, he saw the man in dark clothing.

"Come, boy. I think we have business," he said.

Beran at once became abject. Looking up fearfully, he said, "I've done no wrong, master. I'm only a poor boy making his way to the Holy Land."

The man laughed softly. It was a good-natured laugh, and his look was friendly, but his grip did not slacken. "I'm pleased to hear it, boy. But you don't look much like a pilgrim to me."

"I'm going there to find my brother."

"Of course you are. And why not make your way in comfort, with money jingling in your purse and rich clothes on your back? Wouldn't you rather ride a fine horse than walk?"

"I have no horse, master. I'm only a poor boy."

"Ah, but I have a horse. And if you do as I say, you'll soon have one, too. I liked that business of pretending you're half crippled and then doing your tricks once you've been fed. You did it very nicely."

"I was hungry, master. I meant no harm," Beran said. The man still had firm hold of his arm. Beran was ready to bolt the instant he felt the grip relax.

The man seemed to know what he was thinking. "You're in no trouble, and I intend you no harm. You're a clever lad. I don't like to see such skill and cleverness wasted cadging a bite of meat and a sip of ale."

"What do you want with me, master?"

"I think we might do well together. I have work
for someone clever. I'm a seller of medicines, rare
ointments, precious syrups, powders of great potency.
I travel from town to town, visit the fairs, sometimes
attend the nobility in their palaces, easing their sufferings and curing their ills. It's a fine life for one who
wants to see the world and learn its ways, and make
his fortune as he travels. I seek someone who will
serve me faithfully and assist me in my work. In return, I will teach him the secrets of my art and put gold
in his purse." The man's voice had deepened as he
spoke, and there was a lilt to his words, as if he were
addressing a crowd. He released Beran's arm and
stepped back. "There you are, boy, you're free to run
off if you like. I wish to have no one serve me but of
his own free will."

Beran hesitated. The way to the door was clear, and
he was quick. He could get away easily now, but his
interest had been captured. He had not followed everything the man said, but he knew that he was being
offered the chance of riches by serving him. He spoke
like a clever man, and to judge from his clothing and
his manner, he was prosperous. To serve such a man
was better than traveling with pilgrims, and safer than
making his way alone.

"What would you have me do, master?"

"No more than you did tonight."

"Only that?"

"In time, you'll learn other things. But for the present, you need do only what you did."

"Then I'll serve you, master."

The man smiled at him, and his smile was warm and reassuring. Had Beran not seen such smiles before, he would have trusted this man with his life.

3

The
Charlatans

His voice boomed out over the clamor of the market square, and people began to drift toward the man in black. He stood on a small, sturdy chest that raised him above their heads. On the ground before him lay a square of dark cloth bearing an assortment of glass vials.

"Worthy friends, beloved benefactors, I salute you!" he said, opening his arms as if to embrace the gathering crowd. "Gian of Venezia has come home at last! After years of study and far travel, I have returned to bring the blessings of long life and good health to the people of the city that sheltered me and showed me kindness when I was a homeless boy." His audience looked at him and at one another in doubt, for no one recognized him. But he proceeded to astonish them by recalling incidents from long ago. Pointing to a white-haired man, he said, "You, Ansel the cobbler, gave me shelter during the great snow. You found me shivering in rags on your doorstep, and you took me in and made a place for me to sleep by your stove. Do you remember? You fed me and gave me a warm coat. Thanks to you and your kindness I am alive today." The man gaped at him, then nodded in sudden enthusiastic recognition and turned to those nearby to attest to the memory. "And Damien. Where is Damien the carpenter? You fed me with your own hand when I was too weak to stand. Do you remember, Damien?" An aged man smiled up at him bewildered, vague in memory but prompted to remembrance by the praise and approbation of those around him.

"I remember you with gratitude, one and all, and I have brought you the fruits of my long labor," said the man in black. "In my travels I have been given riches to help men prolong their sickly lives and restore health to those of great age. But I bring you not long life alone, or good health alone. I bring both of these blessings, for who would have the one when he might have both? Who would wish to go on from one year to the next, ever weaker, ever frailer, while his eyes film over, and his teeth loosen and drop out, and his back bends like a drawn bow, and the flesh wastes away from his brittle bones, leaving him like a bundle of dry sticks, chilled by every breeze, scarce able to stand, afraid to walk, failing in memory, bereft of old friends and youthful desires, a mere reeking bag of pain and illness? Who would wish for such a life?" he asked, darting an eager glance from one upturned face to another. "And yet, what is the good of health and strength and a sound body to one who may lose them all before the sun sets? Oh, no, my friends, my old friends, no one can be happy without both." He shook his head slowly, thoughtfully. Then he looked up, smiled benevolently, and spread his arms wide. "And I have come to bring these blessings to you and your children. Good health, that makes the poorest man richer than a king! Long life, that makes the rich man wise and happy!"

He stepped down from his rostrum, allowing his listeners a moment to whisper to one another while he rearranged the vials on the cloth. Then he ascended once again, cleared his throat, and announced, "I, Gian of Venezia, was a pupil of the famed Scorrachina, the ancient, the knowing, she who has healed popes and kings, emperors and sultans. All wise men know her name and her works. For many years, more years than you would believe, I studied with Scorrachina, learning secrets known to none but the great healer herself, for in her centuries of life she has traveled the world, seeking that knowledge once possessed by the ancients but lost with the burning of Troy and the fall of Rome, lost with the decay of ancient empires buried under obliterating sands, lost in the flight and scattering of the learned before the barbarians. Scorrachina sought those secrets. . . ." He paused and leaned forward, drawing the crowd to him with his expectant glances, and at last said, "Unlike all who sought before, she found them."

He stepped down once again, and took a vial of cloudy liquid from where it lay on the black cloth. Mounting the chest, he raised the vial high for all to see. "Here is the distillation. Here is the secret so long lost. I bring it to you. And not only do I bring you health and length of days, I bring strength and beauty to make joyous a long lifetime. Remember Helen, the fabled Helen. Her beauty was such that she drew an army of kings to fight for her before the walls of Troy, and she was as beautiful at the end of a long life as she was on the day that the heroes of ancient Greece vied for her hand. Remember the queen of the Nile, Cleopatra, who bedazzled Caesar himself when she was a young girl and whose beauty, undiminished half a century later, led Mark Antony to abandon all other loyalties and defy the might of Rome. Whence came such beauty?" He turned the vial so that it caught the morning light, and said, "I hold the secret in my hand."

He swept the crowd with his glance, beckoned, and lowered his voice, drawing them closer. "Not only beauty, I said, but strength of mind and body. Remember Odysseus, wiliest and cleverest of men, he who outwitted the gods themselves and conceived the plan that brought down the walls of Troy, Odysseus, the great deceiver who was never deceived by mortal man. Remember Achilles, boldest of warriors, invulnerable save for a single spot of flesh on his heel. He was made proof against all weapons, it is said, by being dipped into the waters of the river Styx by his mother, the goddess Thetis, and was slain at last only by a poisoned arrow from the bow of Hercules himself that stuck him on the unprotected spot. So goes the legend among those who do not possess the truth. But I tell you, Achilles was not bathed in the Styx; he was bathed in water in which three drops, three drops only, of this elixir— But who is this?''

He paused at sight of the ragged boy who had squirmed through the press to fall prostrate before him. Unable to rise, the boy reached out with one hand, the other being twisted and drawn close to his breast, and cried out, "Gian of Venezia, help me! I beg you, heal me!''

He fell to his knees beside the boy, raised him up tenderly, and said, "Who are you? What do you ask of me?''

In faltering tones, which nevertheless carried well into the crowd, the boy told his tale. Ridden down and left to die in the road, he had recovered only to live as a cripple, his left side withered and paralyzed. He had heard of the healer and his wonderful potions, and followed him from town to town in pursuit, but always arrived too late. He clutched Gian's cloak with his good hand and said, "You are my only hope! I was told of the wonders you performed in Cairo, and how you healed the bishop of Milan. I vowed to follow you even across the world."

Gian looked down on the boy, then up at the circle of anxious faces that surrounded them. His eyes filled with tears. "It is true, I have been privileged to help some at Cairo and in Milan and elsewhere in the world. But, my boy, I am only an agent. I have no power of my own. I dare not promise you a cure. It is the elixir that heals, and the elixir is potent and dangerous. Scorrachina herself said, 'I will cure all ill, if it be God's will.' Some will be cured, but some will be lost. The elixir can harm as well as heal."

"How can the wondrous elixir harm me?" the boy asked.

"It is meant for the young." Gian turned to the onlookers and extended his hands, as if in appeal, as he explained, "One drop each day, for three consecutive days, on the tongue of a girl just one year old, and she will grow up to be as beautiful and as pure as an angel. Wash a boy of the same age for three consecutive days in water containing a single drop of the elixir, and he will become a man immune to weapons and illness. But for adults, the effects are different. For a grown man or woman, the elixir is a grave danger. I myself would refuse to take it even at the point of death, for I am no longer young. No indeed, my good people. On St. Stephen's day I will be fifty-nine years old."

There were murmurs and some shouts of disbelief. The man in black had not a white hair on his head or in his neatly trimmed beard, and his face was unlined. He did not look to be half the age he claimed.

"I see that some of you do not believe me. Very well," he said with a careless shrug. "I assure you, my friends, there are other potions than the elixir, and I know them well. But it is not yet time to speak of such things. No, the elixir might have a terrible effect on any but an infant. If I gave it to this poor boy, I might endanger his life."

The boy reached out, imploring. "I accept the danger. Only help me."

Gian looked about him. He ran a hand through his thick, dark hair. In an agonized voice, he cried, "What shall I do?"

"Give him the elixir!" A man shouted. Others quickly picked up the cry, which grew to an uproar, drowning out the few dissenting voices.

"Very well," said Gian when the outcry had subsided. "And if it be that the lad must die, let us pray that his suffering has brought him close to God. May his death be as sweet as a saint's passing, with fragrance and light, and peace of body and soul, and a vision of the Heavenly City." Gian bowed his head and knelt with clasped hands in a silent show of piety.

Rising and crossing himself, he removed his cloak and laid it over the boy. This done, he climbed on the chest. Raising his hands above his head, he said in a resounding voice, "Pray with me! As I was once a poor helpless boy in this very city, so this boy comes to me for help, and I must give it, whatever my fears and misgivings! You will have it so!"

The crowd cheered and shouted "We will, we will!" and "Cure him!" and other words of encouragement as he descended to kneel at the boy's side. Taking the vial from his jacket, he raised the cripple's head and allowed a single drop to fall on his tongue; then he laid the boy's head back and drew the cloak close around him.

For a moment nothing happened. The crowd pressed closer, watching in silence. The boy lay motionless as stone. Then he drew a deep breath, loudly and hoarsely. He moaned and began to shake his head from side to side. His body shook convulsively, he cried out, and then he was still. Gian knelt over him, holding tightly to the boy's shoulders.

The boy's eyes opened, and he raised his head. He blinked. "The horseman!" he cried, and flinging the cloak aside, he threw up his hands protectively before his face—both his hands, and the one that had been paralyzed moved as swiftly and supply as the other.

Gian started to his feet with a shout of joy. The boy rubbed his eyes and looked up at him, and Gian extended a hand to help him rise. The boy climbed to his knees, then to his feet. He took an unsteady step toward his benefactor, then fell forward to embrace him. The crowd erupted.

Gian stepped away and the boy stood firmly, unaided. He moved his arm and flexed his fingers. He took a few slow and cautious steps. Then he threw himself at the feet of the man in black and cried, "Thank you, Master Gian, thank you! I can walk again!"

Raising him up, Gian said, "It is not my doing. The elixir has made you whole of body."

The boy looked wonderingly at the hand that had been paralyzed and now moved freely. "Are my limbs truly restored?"

"You are as you were before."

"Before I was trampled, a man taught me to juggle. Is it possible I have regained my skill?"

"Try and see. The elixir is powerful."

The boy looked about, and his eyes fell on the gloves tucked in Gian's belt. "Master, if I may? Your gloves?" he said.

Gian handed him the gloves. The boy rolled each one into a ball, then looked to the crowd. Half a dozen hands held out gloves to him. He took one from a prosperous gentleman, thanked all who had offered, and rolled a third ball. For a moment he hesitated, a look of uncertainty on his face. Gian laid a hand on his shoulder and said, "Trust in the elixir of Scorrachina."

The boy began to juggle, clumsily at first, dropping the makeshift balls on his first two attempts. Gian picked them up each time, speaking words of encouragement. On his third attempt, the boy was able to keep the balls in the air for a full minute.

Gian stood on the chest and raised his hands for silence, for in its enthusiasm the crowd had become noisy. When his voice could be heard by the farthest spectator, he said, "You have seen the potency of the elixir. It is more powerful, and more subtle, than even I know. It will do wondrous things for the young. Because of his youth, this boy was given back the use of his broken limbs and his old skill. But the elixir is meant only for the young. You saw that one drop sufficed for him—had I given him a single additional drop, he might now be dead and shriveled to a mummy. But be of cheer. For those past their youth, I have another kind of help."

Leaving them to ponder his last words, Gian stepped down and took up the vials. "If this boy will assist me—"

"Gladly, master! I will serve you from this day on!" Beran cried.

"Then we will pass among these good people and distribute the elixir. It is my gift to the citizens, in gratitude for their past kindness. I ask nothing in return. The knowledge that your daughters will be beautiful and strong and bear healthy children, and your sons will live long, free of pain and sickness, to be defenders of this great city, is all the reward I seek."

He handed a dozen vials to the boy, and they entered the crowd, which pressed in on them, reaching and clawing. When they had distributed the last vial, Gian struggled back to the center, where he called out, "I have given you all I possess. Share it freely, I urge you. Be generous with one another, as you were generous to me."

"What about the rest of us?" a man cried. "You gave me none." "No, nor I," said a second and a third. Other angry voices arose, and there was arguing and dissension among the onlookers.

Gian raised his hands in a placating gesture, appealing for their attention. "I have not forgotten the rest of you. The elixir was my gift to your children. For those no longer young, I have another kind of aid ... the powders of Scorrachina," he said, holding up a packet he drew from his sleeve. "But these, my friends, I cannot give you, much as I wish to. The ingredients are rare, and must be purchased at great price. The powders are made of samples gathered from every corner of the world by Scorrachina herself: the dried blossoms of an Afric tree that blooms once in a hundred years; the roots of a luminous plant that grows only on an island at the edge of the world; the scales of a fish that lives in the belly of Leviathan . . ."

Gian went on to list the exotic ingredients of the powder and tell of its remarkable powers—provided it was prepared to an exact prescription at the proper phase of the moon, and allowed to steep for exactly sixty-one days, and properly stored, and applied only in accordance with his intricate instructions. These necessities observed, it would heal all wounds, cure all ills, and turn pain, sickness, and impotence into hardihood and vigor. Gian himself, an old man with the strength and freshness of youth, stood as living proof of its efficacy. And for this wondrous powder, which kings and princes had purchased with more gold and jewels than would fill the square in which they stood, Gian asked not all their goods, nor half, nor even a tithe, but only two silver staters—a price that all could afford, so all might buy.

And all, or very nearly all, did.

That evening Gian and Beran dined with Ansel the cobbler and spent the night in a chamber over his shop. It was small but snug and dry, and distant from the family's quarters. They could talk without fear of being overheard.

"The word will spread. Tomorrow I'll sell as many powders as I did today. And the silversmith has asked me to look at his son. He'll pay well," said Gian.

"Can you cure him?" Beran asked.

"Possibly. I'll surely do the poor lad less harm than others have done."

"Were you really a boy in this city?"

Gian laughed. "I've never set foot in it before. And I'll never set foot in it again, once we've milked all we can get out of it."

"But you knew those people. And they remembered you."

"I spent last night at the inn, listening and asking a question or two. It's easy enough to learn the names of a few respectable citizens old enough to forget what happened fifty years before."

"So you made up the story about their saving your life."

"No man denies a good deed, especially when it's proclaimed before his neighbors. By now, this cobbler and the other fellow, the carpenter, probably remember every detail of their charity to me." He laughed again, softly, a laugh of quiet amusement. "I wager that half the old men and women in the city are remembering the kindnesses they did me when I was a poor homeless lad. People are as quick to remember the good things they didn't do as they are to forget the bad things they did. There's a lesson for you, lad."

Gian busied himself counting his profits, chuckling to himself from time to time. When he was finished, he pushed a little mound of coins to Beran, saying,

"Keep these. I'll hold the rest. We'll buy you some new clothes before we leave."

"Will I travel with you now?"

"Of course you will. You told the crowd you'd serve me, didn't you?" He laughed and poked Beran in the ribs. "Now that the wonderful elixir has cured you, you can juggle again. Can you do conjuring, or other tricks?"

"Some. Not many."

"Well, you'll learn. I had a dwarf who used to juggle and sing and do acrobatics. Haincelin was his name. He knew all sorts of tricks, but he had a foul temper. He stabbed a man in a tavern one night, and was hanged for it."

Beran remembered the raider he had killed, back at his village. "I never want to stab anyone."

"I hope you never have to. Don't want you getting yourself hanged. You did well today, Beran."

Beran drifted off to sleep feeling very comfortable. He had made more in a single day with Gian—as the man now called himself—than he had made in all his years of juggling, and tomorrow he would make even more. He was to have a new outfit, and soon they would be off to see new places. He had found a good life.

They left the city three days later. Gian had treated the silversmith's son, who was in agony from stomach pains, and left him feeling slightly better. The silversmith was beside himself with gratitude. Gian had a fine time along the way mimicking the old man's fulsome speech of thanks.

They stopped at a series of fairs, where Beran juggled while Gian, now calling himself Wagner of Wittenberg, sold his medicines. The take was small, and when the summer ended, Gian announced that they would soon visit another city and have Beran play a sufferer once again.

"What if they've heard of us?" he asked.

"We'll be different people. This time you'll be blind and I'll be . . . I'll be the great Eliodas of Antioch. I'll heal you with the miraculous Greek salve prepared from a lost recipe of the Israelites and rediscovered by a disciple of Galen."

"But if anyone recognizes us . . ."

"You worry too much. We're doing well. You can't expect to make more money unless you're willing to take more risks."

Beran could put up no argument, even though most of what they made remained in Gian's hands. They separated a few miles from the city, Gian riding in ahead, Beran waiting a day before slipping into the city in beggar's rags.

Gian had changed his mind about Beran's disguise. Blindness was hard to feign without long practice, and there were too many fraudulent blind men about. The boy was to pretend to be a mute. They worked out a sign language between them, to account for Gian's comprehension of the boy's inhuman moans and howls. Gian was in great spirits, full of ideas and suggestions. It was clear that he took almost as much delight in deception itself as he did in the wealth that flowed from it.

Once again they enjoyed success. This time, for greater credibility, Gian decided that Beran's cure must be only partial. His speech was restored but his voice remained harsh, and he had to strain to utter one word at a time. This seemed to impress the onlookers even more than a miraculous total cure, and spur their desire for the efficacious salve of the doctor from Antioch. No one recognized them, no one challenged them, and for days afterward, Gian exulted in their success and taunted Beran for his timidity.

"Someone's bound to recognize us one of these days," Beran protested.

"Beran, my boy, you're like an old peasant woman, seeing the devil everywhere. You'll never be a rich man."

"I want to stay alive."

"If it will make you comfortable, we'll disguise ourselves. I'll whiten my beard, and stoop over. Oh, yes, yes," Gian said, laughing at the prospect. His voice rose and cracked. "I'll be a patriarch from the far Arabian deserts, with the healing salts of Solomon and St. Luke. And you . . . ah, we'll fix you up with a lovely mess of sores and scabs, and cure you miraculously."

In the fall, they went to markets and fairs, where Beran juggled and Gian, under an assortment of names, sold his powders, potions, and salves. Gian talked of nothing but his next spectacular cure, and worked out elaborate variations on his scheme. Beran was ill at ease with all of them.

Gian laughed at his misgivings. There had in fact been only two troubling encounters, and Gian had handled them easily. When a knot of men in one city began to cry out "Fraud" and "Charlatan" and accuse them of swindling honest men and women, Gian denounced his accusers as blasphemers and turned the crowd against them, forcing them to flee. The profits that day were especially good. During the summer, at a fair, men armed with clubs had rushed them, calling Gian a murderer and poisoner. He acted quickly, tossing a generous handful of coins into the crowd. He and Beran had escaped in the wild scramble that followed.

Gian had treated both these incidents as great sport, and Beran, at the time, laughed along with him and thought of them as adventures. But he could not help wondering how long their luck would hold. He was sure that he had seen familiar faces in some recent crowds. He was uncomfortable at the thought of what might happen should they be unable to make their escape.

On their way to a market day, they stopped at an alehouse. Gian liked such places, claiming that one could learn more about the countryside from an evening at a low alehouse than from a month spent with the lord of the land. He quickly made himself at home, joking and singing with the others, exchanging bits of news and rumor about people unknown to Beran.

Left to his own devices, the boy observed the crowd. They did not seem quite so exciting as such people once had. Their talk and their stock of tales were as limited as those of the people in his village had been, and they boasted of foolish things. He saw a man and woman sitting apart in a dark corner, and something about them stirred a memory. He slipped closer to study them unseen, and saw that they were the juggler and the dancer he had seen some years before, when his father had taken him to the fair.

They had changed, and the change shocked him. He remembered a confident and clever man, master of the moment, quick of hand and quick of speech, and he beheld a broken beggar. He remembered a beautiful and graceful woman dressed in finery, and he saw a crone in dirty rags.

The woman noticed him, and cried, "What are you staring at? We've done nothing to you! Leave us alone!"

"I saw you once, at a fair. You danced."

The man turned slowly. "You saw us? You saw my tricks?"

"Yes. You were good. Both of you were very good," Beran said, though he had now seen enough to realize that they were not good at all, except in the eyes of those who had never seen better.

"We were the best. We went to noble houses and were treated with respect. I wore fine clothes and jewels," said the woman. "I danced for princes."

The man held up his hands, and they looked like gnarled roots. The fingers were bent and out of place. He could barely move them. "Peasants did this. May they burn in hell for it. They said I cheated them, smashed my hands, beat us both until we couldn't stand. Dirty ignorant peasants, hating what they can't understand."

"He never cheated anyone. He was too clever for them, and they hated him for it." The woman looked Beran over and smiled a black-toothed smile. "You're a pretty lad. Buy us a drink, there's a good fellow. Let's have a pot of ale together, like old friends."

Beran laid three pennies before the woman. She reached out and grabbed his wrist. "You have money, do you? How much have you got? I can show you a good time, lad. I know tricks these village sluts don't know."

"No," he said, jerking free, repelled by her ugliness and her sour breath.

"What's the matter, boy? Afraid of the ladies?"

"No. I'm not afraid."

"Maybe you're a little lady yourself, serving your master's wishes. Is that why you're afraid of me?"

"No!"

"Run away, little lady!" she cried, laughing and pointing at him. "Run to your master. He'll protect you from the wicked women, he will."

Beran ran from the alehouse and stood by the tree where Gian's horse was tied. He was confused and frightened. He had felt sorry for the juggler and the dancer and wanted to help them, and now he hated them, but still he pitied them their suffering, pitying them all the more because their fate might befall him one day, if Gian's tricks failed. He did not want the woman—she was old and ugly, crawling with lice, and she stank like a kennel—but he had helped them. He did not understand why she had said those things about him.

A rain barrel stood outside the alehouse, brimful after the day's showers. Beran went to it and studied his reflection. His pale hair was closely cropped. He had a thin face, with a pointed chin. His nose was straight, his brows already furrowed, his cheekbones prominent. He did not look like a girl.

"Admiring yourself?" Gian said, and Beran started at the voice.

"No. I'm just . . . looking."

"I heard that hag. You shouldn't let her ranting bother you."

"But the things she said . . ."

Gian laughed. "You're no little lady, I can tell her that much. I saw you with the girl at the inn the other night. And the two in town last week."

"Why did she say such things?"

"You were generous, so she thought you were weak. You were a fool to give them anything. You can't be kind to people like that."

"I remembered them from a fair. Did you see what happened to him?"

"I don't care what happens to the likes of him. His kind just make trouble for the rest of us. He got no more than he deserved, whatever it was. I've seen him working. He was a clumsy ape. A child could see how he was cheating."

"The people smashed his hands and beat him."

"Bound to happen to an oaf like that sooner or later. Come on, now, forget your old companions and let's be on our way."

"They're not my old companions!"

"Then they'll be the easier to forget. There's a festival four days' ride from here, and I plan to perform a miraculous cure on you. We ought to do well if we can get there while everyone still has money to spend."

Beran slept poorly that night. He awoke from a bad dream and heard a distant bell toll eleven. He lay awake, thinking of the juggler's broken hands. He remembered the faces in the crowd that seemed so familiar, and thought of the festival and what might happen there if he and Gian were recognized.

Beran was not helpless. He had his dagger, though he had never used it, remembering too vividly the sensation of driving a blade into a man's body. He had seen his share of violence, and Gian had shown him how to defend himself using thumb, knee, and elbow, tankard or stool or anything that happened to be within reach. But against an angry mob, he would have no chance.

When he was sure that Gian was asleep, he rose, gathered his things, and slipped away. It was dangerous to travel in the night, and he was frightened. But the thought of what might happen if he stayed made him determined to go.

4

The
Apprentice

Beran had learned much in his travels with Gian. His juggling ability had improved, and now when he performed in a tavern or at a fair, he was able to amuse the onlookers as much with what he said as with what he did. He felt more confident. He dreamed up fanciful names for himself, and imaginary histories, and drew on all the tales he heard to create adventures that brought cries of wonder and loud laughter from his listeners.

Their largess, he found, was not always equal to their appreciation. It was easier to make people cheerful than to make them generous.

He traveled with pilgrims whenever he could. They were sometimes dull company, but of all those on the road, they were the least likely to be attacked by robbers or to steal from one of their number. Some of them were generous with their food, but one could never count on that. Beran looked for groups with a few aged members, or someone on crutches or in a litter traveling in search of a cure. Such groups traveled at a slower pace, and did not leave him footsore and exhausted at the end of the day.

While he was with a large, easygoing company on their way to the shrine of a local saint, he had his first meeting with a penitential pilgrim. He had sometimes seen them on the road, solitary figures, ragged and filthy, often bent under the weight of chains and fetters, hair and beard long and tangled from their years of wandering. Such men were the worst of sinners. Though they were on pilgrimage, the pilgrimage was no proof that they had repented their sins, for it was enforced and not voluntary. And even if they were truly penitent, the very fact of their pilgrimage meant that they were not yet reconciled to God and the Church.

Yet these pilgrims, through their great sufferings, might achieve a blessed state. Julian had told him of one man, a powerful lord who had slain his own brothers in a drunken rage and been condemned to lifelong exile with fetters on his wrists and ankles and an iron collar about his neck. He had dragged his way from shrine to shrine, and never received a sign of forgiveness, for his own heart was unmoved. Then, in his fortieth year of wandering, when he reached the Holy Land and waded into the Jordan, the chains and collar had fallen from him and he had emerged from the river in snow-white garments, as one newly baptized. That very night he died a peaceful and holy death. Julian had not seen this with his own eyes, but he had heard it from one whose word could not be doubted.

The man Beran now saw was a sorry figure. He lay by the roadside, unmoving, and when all had passed him by, Beran returned. He had no clear purpose in mind other than to study more closely this wretched figure.

As he came near, the man called out weakly, "I am Gilbert, a sinner. I am Gilbert of Sanlac, a sinner. Pray for me."

"I will pray for you. What was your sin?"

"I slew a priest. I struck the bishop who accused me and denounced him as a liar. Pray for me."

"I have said I will. Here," Beran said, holding out his water bottle. Gilbert reached for it with a hand like an eagle's claw, gaunt and bony, the fingers seamed with filth, the nails like yellowed talons. His face, behind a thicket of matted hair, was scarcely more than a skull with vacant eyes set deep in red-rimmed sockets. His nose, an almost fleshless blade, was raw and scabbed.

Gilbert sipped at the water bottle and then thrust it back. "I must take no more."

"I can give you some food."

"No. I eat only once a day."

"Where are you bound?"

The sunken eyes came suddenly alive. "Tours!" Gilbert said in a harsh whisper. "There my penance will end."

"Tours is not many days off."

"For me it has taken years," said the pilgrim. His breath was shallow, and he spoke in short bursts. "Santiago, then Rome . . . Jerusalem at last. But even in the Holy Land I had more to endure. As I knelt before the basilica, I heard a voice. It ordered me to turn back and go to Tours. There my chains will be struck off. My punishment will end."

"Then it is nearly over."

"Yes." He rolled to his hands and knees and struggled to his feet. "I must go. Remember Gilbert of Sanlac, a sinner. Pray for me," he said, and hobbled ahead on unsteady shackled feet.

Beran watched him go, and for a few moments he entertained the thought of following him to Tours so that he might see with his own eyes the chains drop from his ankles. Perhaps Gilbert, too, would be miraculously clad in white. There might be other miracles as well. Angels might appear, or a saint speak. A sick or crippled person might be healed. It would be a fine thing to witness a miracle. He would have something to tell about all his life, and never lack eager listeners.

Beran watched until the hobbling figure was out of sight, then rejoined the company of pilgrims. He spoke of Gilbert to several of them, but no one showed interest in the penitent's story. By evening, Beran himself had ceased to care about Gilbert, or Tours, except as a diverting detail in a story to be told someday.

That night he dreamed of a man all in white, and came awake in the darkness with a sudden start. He could recall no message, no warning voice or exhortation, no summoning gesture, only a single vivid image. If there had been anything more to the dream, it was already gone. He lay awake pondering, straining to bring back details. He could recapture nothing of his dream but the nameless, faceless man in white.

Surely the man was Gilbert of Sanlac, and the dream was a summons to Tours. There could be no other explanation. When at last Beran managed to get back to sleep, it was with the determination to follow Gilbert.

He left the company of pilgrims in the morning, after he had eaten, and started for Tours alone, trusting in the dream vision. If he had been called to Tours, he would be protected on his way.

He kept a leisurely pace. Gilbert, with his shackled ankles, could not move fast, and he did not wish to get ahead of the penitent. He followed him for two days, and then, on the third day, he had an encounter that was to change his plans, and his life, forever.

He came to a town that was celebrating its saint's name day. Outside the walls was a fair, and he stopped to watch and, if opportunity should present itself, to make a bit of money. He saw a gaunt, dispirited black bear put through his paces by a dark little man who barked commands in a strange tongue. A slender lady danced on her hands and contorted herself into impossible postures, squeezing through hoops that seemed too narrow to admit a woman's hand, much less her whole body. And then he came upon the juggler, and knew at once that he had found the one he had long been seeking.

He was a broad, burly man, black-haired and red-faced, looking more like a blacksmith than a juggler. His clothing was plain but well made, the only spot of color the striped sash about his waist. He spoke familiarly to the crowd, as if he were chatting with old friends, and as he took up the brightly painted balls, he addressed them, too, in an ongoing comradely monologue. He spoke softly, confidingly, and Beran, though he had pushed all the way to the front of the crowd, had to strain to follow his words.

"Up you go, there, you too, all of you, up there, quickly now," he said as he tossed up the first three balls. "That's the way, nicely now, that's what I want to see. Well done, nicely done, that's the good fellows. Here, you, get up there with your brothers," he said as he added a fourth ball. Soon a fifth, a sixth, and a seventh joined the arcs that ran between his hands, and the juggler spoke to them as a man would to a

team of well-trained animals. He was affectionate and
yet masterful, familiar yet dominant.

Next he juggled daggers. First he let the crowd test
their points and edges. Beran took one, plucked a hair
from his head and cut it on the edge, then tried the
point on his thumb. These were daggers that could
draw blood at a touch.

The juggler took a serious approach to them. This
time he spoke more firmly, as if he were dealing with
dubious acquaintances who might befriend him or
turn on him, as the mood struck them. "You behave
yourselves now, none of your tricks, do as I tell you
and no nipping at me. There, that's my fine friends,
gleam away, flash and shine and turn, that's the way.
Ah, you're beautiful and you know it, but don't you
go getting nasty. Do as I tell you, smoothly now,
that's the way, that's right. Everyone's watching you,
every eye is on you, and you have to be at your best.
Good, good, you're doing fine, there you go, never
done better."

Beran was delighted. Here was the master who
could teach him the things a juggler had to know, and
help him to be the best. Gilbert of Sanlac vanished
from his mind. This was the summons he wanted to
follow.

The act climaxed with six torches, and this time the
juggler was totally silent. His silence brought a hush
over the audience and drew them closer. Beran

watched intently, observing the juggler's hands and
the placement of his feet, the expression on his face,
the movement of his eyes, everything that might hold
a clue to his smooth and confident performance. He
found no one detail that explained it. All fit together
into a seamless whole, and he cheered with unfeigned
delight when the juggler caught the last torch and
flourished all six of them over his head.

When the crowd had broken up, Beran sought out
the juggler. He found the man sitting by a wagon, a
pot of ale in his hand. When Beran came in sight,
he looked up at the boy without welcome in his expression.

"Teach me how to juggle," Beran said.

"Teach yourself. I'm not a schoolmaster."

"But you're the best. I'll work for you. I need no
money. Just show me how to do the things you do."

The man laughed. "There are things I do that I'd
never teach anyone, for fear we'd both be hanged." He
took a swallow of ale, looked Beran over closely, and
said, "I suppose you can juggle."

Beran drew three balls from his jacket and began.
After a minute, the man said, "Try it with four," and
tossed a wooden ball to him. He worked it in
smoothly, grinning at his own success.

The man smiled and nodded in approval. Then,
still smiling, he suddenly tossed Beran another ball. It
seemed to come out of nowhere. Beran could not

control it, and was barely able to catch the balls before they fell.

"It appears that four is your limit."

"So far," Beran said.

"I can keep eight in the air. It's taken me most of my life to learn that much. Do you know how to bounce them off your knee, and your instep?"

"No," Beran said. He had never even thought of such tricks.

"Have you ever used daggers and torches?"

"No."

"You have a lot to learn."

"I work hard. I practice all the time."

"Even all the time isn't enough if you expect to be any good. It may take you years, working every day, to master a trick, and once you've learned, you'll still have to practice it every day or lose it. How did you learn?"

"I saw a man at a fair. I did what he did until I could juggle three balls, and then I kept practicing until I could manage four."

"Have you ever worked with another juggler?"

"No."

"Well, that's what you'll learn first. I don't want a pupil, but I could do with a partner. If you're a good partner, I'll teach you what I know. By the time I'm too old to keep going, you may be good enough to perform by yourself. What's your name, boy?"

"Beran."

"I've never heard that one before. Where are you from?"

Beran pointed to the west. "That way."

The man laughed and nodded his head. "Run away from your village, have you? What was the matter? Your master too hard on you?"

"I didn't run away! The village was destroyed. I'm the only one left."

"That's as good a story as any. All right, Beran, you'll be my servant, my apprentice, my pupil, whatever you want to call yourself. You can start by fetching water," the man said, indicating the empty bucket with a jerk of his thumb.

"What's your name, master?"

"Call me Sejourne. And be quick with that water."

Beran was off to the nearby stream at once. When he returned, he asked Sejourne, "Are we going to Tours?"

Sejourne looked at him curiously. "Why would I want to go to Tours?"

"It's a great city. It's full of people."

"We're not welcome in Tours. People don't go there to watch the likes of us. They give their money to priests and friars, not jugglers."

Beran thought for just a moment of Gilbert of Sanlac. It would have been a good thing to see his chains fall away, and perhaps witness a miracle. But Sejourne could teach him what he wanted to know. Having found a master, he could not leave him, not even for the possibility of witnessing a miracle. And perhaps there would be no miracle at Tours after all, and he would miss nothing. Whatever happened, he could make something good out of Gilbert's story. That would suffice for now.

Thus began Beran's apprenticeship. Sejourne was a cheerful man and a good traveling companion, but a demanding master. Beran did all the fetching and packing and carrying, cooked and cleaned, helped out in a small way when Sejourne performed, and spent every spare minute practicing under the juggler's hawklike eye.

Sejourne missed nothing. He corrected every motion, demanded repetition after repetition, and was quick to apply a switch to Beran's legs or clout him across the head if the boy seemed to be slackening. Even when Beran was certain that he was perfect, Sejourne had him practice over and over until his arms and neck ached and he was ready to drop from exhaustion.

"You'll never be perfect, but that's no excuse for laziness. Remember that. No matter how good you are, you can be better if you keep working at it," he said whenever Beran was discouraged.

Discouragement came easily in the early days, when work and practice seemed to begin at dawn and go on until the last light faded, and sometimes long after, by firelight. But Beran learned. Before a year was out, he was performing with his master.

At first he was no more than someone to keep the crowd's attention while Sejourne made ready for his next stunt. In time, when Sejourne judged him ready, they worked side by side, but Beran's role was still a minor one. Then Sejourne announced that they would begin to work together with the daggers.

Beran was excited at the prospect when his master explained it, but the experience was quite different. Standing face-to-face with Sejourne and having those sharp and deadly blades sent whirling at him was terrifying. They wore thick pads to protect their chests, but Beran took little comfort from that, imagining a dagger piercing his eye, or plunging into his arm or leg or throat. He managed to get through the first practice session without mishap, but he felt no confidence. Even after weeks of regular practice, and increased speed and smoothness in his performance, Beran still took up the daggers with apprehension.

"Afraid of them, are you?" Sejourne said one day as they rested after a long morning session.

"I'm not afraid," Beran said quickly.

"Anyone who's not afraid of flying daggers is a fool. Are you telling me you're a fool?"

"No. But I'm not really afraid."

Sejourne laughed. "Too bad you can't see the expression on your face when they start coming at you. You look like you've seen the devil."

"I'm concentrating."

"That's good. Now add a little fear. I don't want you shaking in your boots, but I want you to have a healthy respect for the risks. Never let your mind wander, and never get overconfident. Get the least bit careless and you'll be hurt, no matter how good you are."

Beran had no doubt of that.

When Sejourne was satisfied with his skill, Beran was allowed to become a regular performer. He still did most of the work, but Sejourne no longer treated him as a child or servant. He learned to work with torches and hatchets, and on his own he began to try out other objects and devise new techniques. Unlike Sejourne, he worked in absolute silence and total concentration, his face expressionless. Some of the onlookers, he learned, had the impression that his mind was far away, and that he was remote and detached, or even bored. In truth, he was so tightly focused on what he was doing that he forgot everything else.

Sejourne had a good, deep, resounding bass, and he knew songs of all kinds. His repertoire extended from the old tales of love and battle and the legends of Arthur and his knights suitable to hall and castle, to the satirical and sometimes downright seditious songs popular among the working people of the countryside. Beran's voice, though untrained, was pleasing, and once his master had heard the boy sing, he set him to learning songs and ballads and keeping time on a tambour. They traveled for a time with a band of minstrels and tumblers, and Beran had his first chance to see the homes of great and powerful families.

In his childhood he had known the small, rude castle of Sir Morier, more fortress than dwelling, and thought that no more splendid place existed outside of heaven itself. Now he had a glimpse of real magnificence: palaces that sprawled over the whole of a mountaintop, with a score of chambers and a hall that soared high overhead; intricately carved wood, gilded and painted; brightly colored tapestries that told stories of chivalry and enchantment; servants rushing to and fro; lights blazing everywhere. He saw men and women dressed in silk and fine wool, with furs at throat and wrist, rings on their fingers and jewels hung about their necks. He saw—and smelled and sometimes tasted—foods better than anything he had ever dreamed of. When he sang in the minstrels' gallery, and performed before the high table, his eyes went everywhere, taking everything in and savoring every sight and sound and color.

Sometimes the rewards were generous. One great lord gave each member of their company a silver piece, and the lady of the castle, who had taken special pleasure in Beran's singing, had matched the gift. Another lord presented Sejourne with a splendid doublet and Beran with a cloak and hood of soft wool, even though such benefactions were frowned upon by his almoner, who exhorted him to give to the poor and not to minstrels, jugglers, and flatterers. Almost everywhere they performed, they were well fed and given plenty to drink, but now and then they were turned away hungry and thirsty and empty-handed.

After four years of working together, Sejourne treated Beran as an equal. Now a young man, Beran was indeed his master's equal in skill, and still eager to improve and learn, while Sejourne was content. When Beran began to talk of new feats, Sejourne listened patiently, with mild amusement at the youth's enthusiasm, and then spoke of his own desire to find a place with some great lord, and end his life of wandering.

Sejourne's health was beginning to fail. Sometimes he had a coughing fit in the night, awakening Beran. He was as big and burly as ever, his voice as strong, his appetite as great. He never complained, so Beran suspected nothing. But one day, at a fair, Sejourne began to cough uncontrollably while they were working with the daggers, and only the padding under his doublet saved him from injury. It was a long time before the coughing subsided and Sejourne could talk. Beran noticed for the first time that there were flecks of blood at the corners of his mouth.

"We can't work as partners anymore, Beran. It's too dangerous," he said that night as they sat by the fire.

"I'll work alone for a time, while you rest. You'll get better."

Sejourne shook his head. "I've been getting worse

and worse for the past year. Longer than that. Rest won't cure me, though I'll be glad for it. One of these days you'll have to leave me with the monks. They'll feed me, and pray over me. . . . Maybe they'll even save my soul. They'll have a job of it." He laughed at that thought, and the laughter brought on a paroxysm of coughing. Beran could only look on helplessly while his master, his friend and partner, struggled for breath.

Sejourne seemed to recover in the next few days and they traveled on, but things were different now. Beran was the juggler, and Sejourne did the conjuring tricks. He was quick to regain his skill with the cups and balls, and his monologue was now directed at his audience. The swiftness of his hands and the smoothness of his speech had them mystified, and even Beran was often surprised at the feats his master performed: making three balls appear in place of one, or turning one into three, or making them all disappear, or turning white balls to black, or black to white, or all of them to flowers or white mice or frogs.

His appreciation for Sejourne's skill did not inspire him to learn it, much to the master's irritation. He practiced the cup-and-ball manipulations dutifully, and became quite skilled at conjuring tricks. But only juggling could absorb his attention totally and command his entire enthusiasm. Sejourne admonished him regularly.

"You've got to learn other skills," he said one day

in exasperation. "If I couldn't do other things, I'd starve."

"If I must learn other things, I will, but I'll wait until I have to. All I want now is to be the best juggler in the world."

"That's a nice, modest ambition."

"I'm willing to work hard."

"You'd better be. You're good, Beran, but you're a long way from the best. And even if you were the best, people don't care. They want to see you do tricks, all kinds of tricks, not just juggling."

"I'll make them watch me. I'll be so good, they'll forget about other tricks."

Sejourne laughed and shook his head. His laughter was more subdued these days. "I wish you luck. You may have to forget about eating."

As winter drew near, Sejourne's cough returned, and his seizures grew worse and more frequent. Beran often thought of leaving him and striking out on his own. Sejourne had nothing more to teach him, and his insistence on learning to do what everyone else did was annoying.

Beran did not want to be like all the rest. He knew that he could be better, perhaps the best of all, and he longed for a master who would help him to realize his ambition. There must be someone better, someone who could teach him what he wanted to know, a great master who would help him achieve his goal, and not force him into the smaller mold of common tricksters.

But whenever he made up his mind to leave, he thought of the good times he and Sejourne had had together, and the kindness the man had shown him over the years. He was not greedy, like Gian, or always angry, like the father Beran could now scarcely picture in his mind. He had taught well, and when Beran was sick, he had nursed him back to health. Now that Sejourne was the sick one, Beran owed him the same. The monks would care for him, but they were not his old friends and companions. It would not be the same.

Beran stayed, but he kept his eyes and ears open for news of a better opportunity.

5

The
Pact

Late in the year, they had made enough money to stay in town for the worst of the winter. Their room was small and dirty, but they had it all to themselves and could keep a fire burning day and night. Sejourne's cough was infrequent and less severe. He began to look and sound more like his old self, and Beran put aside his ideas of going out on his own.

Sejourne spent much of the time working at a pastime popular in the inns and alehouses, a guessing game played with straws. He and Beran played every day, and Sejourne developed great skill at guessing how many straws his partner held.

"You have to think like the other fellow. You have to know what he thinks, and what he thinks you think, and what he thinks you think he thinks. Then you can win every time," Sejourne said.

"If you win all the time, people will say you cheat."

"I said you *can* win every time, not that you should. You mustn't be greedy."

"Even if you're not greedy, people accuse you," Beran said. He had not forgotten the mangled hands and battered face of the old juggler. There had been a tense moment only a few nights before that recalled it to him all too vividly.

Sejourne seemed to read his thought. "That miller was a drunken fool. He shut up quick enough when I shook my fist in his face."

"What if the others had believed him?"

"Don't worry so much. As long as you make the other fellow believe he's got a chance, you'll have no trouble. You have to lose on purpose now and then, and when you win, you have to buy ale for everyone."

"You won't end up with much."

"You'll have enough. You'll never go hungry, or sleep under a tree in the rain."

Sickness had changed Sejourne's ideas. He was more concerned about food and shelter than he had been before, and talked much about the need for money. Beran had no inclination to argue with him. He spent most of his time seated before the fire, practicing. Sejourne observed him closely, but said nothing. At last he gave in to his curiosity.

"What are you doing?" he asked one evening.

"Juggling."

"You've got nothing in your hands."

Beran stopped, grinned, and held out his hand. In it lay three dried peas.

"You're a great fool, Beran, surely."

"What's foolish about juggling peas? It's very difficult."

With a dismissive swipe of his hand, Sejourne said, "I heard of a man who taught himself to juggle millet seeds. Year after year he practiced, until he could keep a dozen at a time in the air. A great lord heard of his skill and had him perform at his court. But he could see nothing, only the movement of the juggler's hands, so he turned him out with a purse of millet seeds for his reward. People pay you because you put on a show for them. Only a fool juggles something no one can see."

"I don't care what people can see. I'm not doing it for them, I'm doing it for myself, to be better. That's all I want."

"I know, I know. You want to be the best."

"I do, and I will be."

"How could you ever know if you were the best? The world is a big place. There might be someone in India or Cathay ten times better than you. There might be a lot of people."

"I'd know. It's so important to me that I'd know."

"What's so important about it? You can be good without being the best."

Beran could not explain why he felt such urgency. He knew that it was so, and he accepted it. "It's just important. I'd give anything to be the best in the world."

A sudden gust of wind made the flames dance and sent embers scattering. The door creaked on its hinges. Sejourne hitched closer to the fire and said, "That's easy to say. You have nothing to give."

"I'll give whatever I've got. All I've got," Beran said. He thought of the little treasure he had given to the monks when he was young and had no ambition to drive him, and he regretted his foolish impulse. Another gust of wind made him look to the door and the shutters, and move his own stool nearer the fire.

After a silence Sejourne said, "Maybe we'll have a good year."

"Maybe," Beran said halfheartedly.

"We could go to Tours. Remember when you came to me and asked to be taught? You wanted to go to Tours then."

"You didn't. Why do you want to go now?"

Sejourne shrugged and stared into the fire. "No special reason. It's a big city. We might do well there." Without looking at Beran, he asked, "Why did you want to go to Tours?"

"I thought I'd see a miracle."

"Do they announce miracles in advance these days?"

"I met a man on the road, a penitent. He thought there might be . . . It was nothing. I didn't know anything then." Beran felt himself coloring. He had inquired of every pilgrim he met for many years following his encounter with Gilbert of Sanlac, and none of them had heard of a miracle at Tours. Gilbert's name, and his fate, were unknown.

Sejourne reached out and placed his hand on Beran's shoulder. "Cheer up. Maybe you'll see a miracle yet."

The next day, in the high street, Beran passed an old man in plain, dark clothing who smiled and nodded to him. He looked away quickly and did not return the greeting. Later he described the man to Sejourne, but his partner could not identify him, only suggesting that he might be someone who had enjoyed a past performance and happened to recognize him. This was what Beran feared, remembering his days with Gian. But he did not see the old man again, and no angry accusers came forward. Sejourne's explanation seemed the likely one, and Beran gave no more thought to the encounter.

When the first green appeared, they were on the road again, making their leisurely, roundabout way to Tours. Beran performed at every opportunity, but now he performed alone. Sejourne restricted his activity to the inns and taverns, where he played the game of straws every evening. He always won, but his winnings were not immoderate and he managed to leave the other players, even those who had lost heavily, with the impression that he had barely come out ahead.

Several times, Beran thought he saw the old man in the crowd when he was juggling, but it was always a sidelong glimpse, half-seen and uncertain. Whenever he looked directly, the man was not there.

He decided to say nothing to his partner. The world was full of old men, he told himself, and most of them wear dark clothing, and they all enjoy seeing a good juggler.

At an inn one evening, while Sejourne was playing the game of straws, Beran sat by himself in a quiet corner. He had had a busy day, with little sleep the night before, and was tired. He yawned and rubbed his eyes and settled back to rest, but a sudden breeze from the door chilled him and he sat up, blinking and shivering. He saw an old man seated in a shadowy alcove along the opposite wall. The man raised a hand in greeting.

"You recognize me, don't you, my lad?" he said. His voice was kindly, his manner pleasant.

"I can't see your face."

"You don't have to see my face, do you? You know what I look like."

"You've been in the crowd, watching me, haven't you?"

"Oh, many times. And you know why I'm here, too."

Beran had heard of the old men who sought out young boys, and he wanted nothing to do with them. But this man seemed to read his mind. "It's nothing like that, and you know it," he said. "Think back to what you've said. You've made an offer, and I'm here to accept it."

"I made you no offer. I've never even spoken to you."

"Not directly, perhaps. But I heard what you said. I hear everything that concerns me. You wish to be the greatest juggler in the world, the greatest ever. Is that not so?"

"Yes. And I will be."

"Indeed you will, if you agree to my terms."

Beran leaned forward eagerly. This was good fortune indeed. "Can you teach me?"

Shaking his head, laughing softly, the old man said, "Oh, no, no. I am not a teacher. Nothing so slow as all that. I will make you the greatest juggler in the world in no more time than it takes to say the words. And all I ask in return is something you value very cheaply. From what I have seen, you place no value on it at all."

Beran felt a sudden twinge of fear. He raised a hand before him and shrank away from the old man. "Who are you?"

"It is foolish to ask a question to which you know the answer. You know who I am and what I want, and I have told you what I offer in exchange."

"No!" Beran sprang up and backed away, toward the main room of the inn. He looked for Sejourne. When he glanced back, the old man was gone. Shaken, he pushed his way in among the onlookers to the game of straws, heartened by company, even that of strangers.

Sejourne was slightly ahead, but now he began to win steadily. The two dark, thin-faced merchants reached their loss limit and dropped out of play. Only three players remained.

Sejourne was first to guess. He drew his closed fist from behind his back, laid it on the table, and studied the other two. Their faces were set with determination, but Beran knew that they could not outwit his partner. The redhead with the stringy beard banged his fist down on the table. The big, bald drover deliberated for a time, and would have taken longer had Redbeard not snapped at him. Looking uncomfortable, the drover laid his closed fist on the table.

"Seven," Sejourne said.

Redbeard looked at him with murder in his eyes. He glanced at the bald man, and then he hissed, "Six," and followed with an oath.

The drover frowned, ran his hand over his smooth scalp, and at last hazarded, "Five."

Sejourne opened his hand to reveal the two straws lying on his palm. Redbeard threw his two straws down with disgust. The bald man counted their straws, looked bemusedly at the three in his own hand, and dropped them on the table. Sejourne reached out and drew the jumble of coins in the center of the table to him, adding them to those already heaped before him.

"Another game?" he asked.

"I'll not play against you anymore," Redbeard said, rising. "You read my mind, I swear you do."

"Don't begrudge a man his luck. It was all going your way earlier on. You should have quit then."

As the man pushed his way through the circle of onlookers, muttering, one of them said to Sejourne, "How do you do it?"

"Concentration," Sejourne said, tapping his forehead. "That, and good luck, and you'll win all the time."

"I always concentrate," the drover protested.

"Then all you need is luck. One day it will come."

With the game over, and Sejourne making no move to treat them to drinks, the crowd began to drift off into the dark corners of the inn, murmuring among themselves. Beran was surprised. It was Sejourne's custom to buy drinks for everyone, players and onlookers alike, when he won. He had done so on every occasion, without fail; yet tonight he hunched like a miser over his winnings and looked at everyone with suspicion. Beran sensed no danger in these people. They would drink and grumble and curse the winner for his luck, but do nothing. All the same, it was an inexplicable change in Sejourne's careful methods.

Their chamber was small, with a sloping ceiling. It stank like a ferret's den. It was barely possible to stand erect and unpleasant to breathe deeply. They had to crawl into pallets that lay on the floor next to the wall, and there they found themselves staring up at the rough underside of the thatching scarcely a hand's breadth away. The fleas were quick to welcome them.

"Why didn't you buy drinks for the crowd tonight?" Beran asked.

"Why waste money on them?"

"It would have been a good idea. You won a lot."

Sejourne smiled and held up a bulging purse. "I won it all. I took everything they had."

"You've never done that before. Is it wise?"

"I did it honestly. If they're foolish enough to play against a master, they can pay for the privilege. I've taught them a valuable lesson."

"You and I know you won it honestly, but they'll all say you cheated."

"Let them say what they like. I wasn't the one trying to cheat. Why are you suddenly so concerned about a lot of foolish strangers?"

Beran thought of telling him of the old man's visit, but decided against it, reluctant to bear Sejourne's derision. "I'm concerned about what they might do to you and me."

Sejourne drew his dagger and held it before him. "Let them try. No man will take what I've won honestly."

Beran did not press the matter further. He was surprised, and a bit frightened, by the sudden change in his partner, and thought it best to let the matter drop and hope that a night's sleep would restore Sejourne's old manner.

They were on their way at first light. They had not traveled for an hour when two men stepped from the woods on the side of the path, the red-bearded gambler and another man whom they had not seen before. Redbeard held a short spear. The other carried a cudgel in one hand and a dagger in the other. They took up position on either side of the path, and Sejourne halted at the sight of them. Beran dropped his pack and moved close to his partner's side. Sejourne was bigger than either of the attackers and stronger, even though his strength was less than it once had been. If he could get close enough to strike, he was capable of overcoming them.

"I want the money you stole from us last night," Redbeard said.

"I stole nothing. I won it."

"You cheated. You kept losing and losing so we'd bet more, and then you cheated us out of everything."

Sejourne laughed. "What about the wax on your palm, and the straws you tried to hide between your fingers?"

"That's a lie!" Redbeard cried.

"Swallow your loss, cheat, and don't try to blame it on others."

Redbeard took a step closer and jabbed the spear at Sejourne. "Throw down the money or I'll rip you open."

Sejourne reached for his dagger, but Redbeard was too close and moved too quickly. The spear caught Sejourne in the chest before he could draw the dagger from the scabbard. Beran stood frozen, and only when the other man lunged at him did he react. He drew his own dagger and in the same motion slashed out wildly. The man cried out and covered his face with both hands, and Beran turned and ran.

He could hear heavy steps behind him, closing in. He tore through the clinging undergrowth, stumbling and staggering, but managed to keep on his feet until at last he tripped and went sprawling. The dagger fell from his hands, and he scrambled to snatch it up as the steps closed in. Desperate, terrified, he rolled over and thrust up his dagger, gripping it firmly in both hands. He wanted only to frighten off the man at his heels and give himself time to escape, but he had misjudged the distance. Redbeard threw himself on him, hands outstretched for the boy's throat, and Beran saw the sudden terror in the man's face as he glimpsed, too late, the waiting blade. It slid into his chest directly under the breastbone.

Redbeard clawed at Beran's throat, but his grip was feeble and ineffective, and fell away almost at once. Beran pushed him off and poised for a time on his knees in the grass, gasping and emitting small, wordless groans of horror. There was no blood on his hands or his doublet, but when he crept closer and drew his dagger from the man's chest, blood began to seep forth. He shuddered, and felt for a moment that he would be sick, but the sensation passed. He climbed to his feet and gazed numbly down at the dead man. Redbeard, so menacing moments ago, now looked small and shrunken and pitiful, lying with one hand at his side, the other extended with hooked fingers, his face twisted in anger, his eyes open and staring blankly into the sun.

"Now you're alone," said a familiar voice.

Beran turned and cried out at the sight of the old man. He was seated on a fallen tree within arm's reach.

"What are you doing here? Are you with them?"

"Of course not. You know I'm your friend. I assumed you'd be passing this way, and I wanted to continue our conversation. I have nothing to do with this lot. You acquitted yourself quite bravely, I must say."

"He fell on my blade."

"Of course. Happily, you had the presence of mind to be prepared for his fall."

"I didn't mean to kill him."

"He meant to kill you, and I suspect he would not have done so as quickly and mercifully as you did him. Do not trouble yourself over such a creature. Think of the future. You're on your own now, without a master or a protector, or a single friend, except for me. But for the few pennies in your purse, you have nothing. What will you do?"

Beran covered his face with his hands. He sighed deeply and said in a voice barely audible, "I don't know."

"Have you forgotten your ambition? If you were what you hope to be, you would be well provided for. Protected by the great, adored by the commons, envied by all. Men would give you wealth, women would offer you love, people would honor you and praise you wherever you went. As it is, your life may be difficult . . . and perhaps very short."

Without looking up, Beran said, "What do you want?"

"A trifle. You know what it is."

Beran knew. He had known all along, from the very moment that the old man had greeted him in the street, but had not wanted to admit it to himself. Yet the old man looked so kindly and innocent. His pale face was smooth shaven, his large dark eyes full of sympathy, his white hair snowy in the morning light. He might have been an angel, not the thing he was.

"Yes, I know," Beran said.

The old man nodded, but spoke no word.

"And in return will you make me the greatest juggler in the world, and give me a long life?"

"I will come for you fifty years from this day, and in all that time your skill will never diminish."

Beran climbed to his feet and looked down on the old man, who smiled at him in expectation. "Done," he said.

"A most sensible decision. And what do you offer as a pledge? I must have some proof of your resolve."

Beran held out his right hand. "Here. If I betray you, take it."

"Excellent. Most appropriate." The old man extended a forefinger and touched the palm of Beran's outstretched hand. The boy felt a momentary shock of pain and pulled his hand back instinctively. "Have no fear. I merely sealed our agreement," said the old man. In the center of the palm was a small red mark that had not been there before. "Now let us return and gather your traps. You'll need them."

"But the other robber . . ."

"He is far away by now. Come. See for yourself how much your skill has improved."

Sejourne's body lay face downward where it had

fallen. His arms were flung wide, his hands out-stretched, gripping the grass. Blood pooled out on both sides of his chest. Beran started toward him, to turn him over, but the old man barred his way with his hand.

"You can do nothing for him."

Beran stepped back. He looked down on the unmoving figure for a moment, then took up his pack, which lay untouched where he had let it fall. Sejourne's pack was missing, as was his purse.

"Try out your skill. You will notice some improvement," said the old man. He walked into the woods, beckoning for Beran to follow, and led the way to a clearing.

Beran laid out the contents of his pack and began to juggle, starting simply, with three balls. When eight balls were in the air, he tossed up a dagger, then another, then others, until seven daggers and eight balls whirled in a great flashing arc before him. The old man took up a pair of torches. They burst into flame, and he tossed them to Beran, one by one. He added four more in the same manner, and Beran accepted them, and then the rings.

There in a clearing in the woods, with his partner's body still warm nearby, Beran performed feats that no one before him had ever achieved, or attempted, or even imagined possible. Balls, daggers, torches, and rings danced in the air at his command, obedient to his will. He knelt, and lay in the grass, tossed and caught behind his back, bounced the balls off his knees and instep and the nape of his neck, and all was as simple and easy as the most basic crisscrossing of three balls. He continued longer than he had ever done before, and ended by letting the daggers fall one by one in a line at his feet, catching the rings on his arms and the torches in his hands, while the balls fell in a perfect circle around him.

He whirled the torches overhead, laughing aloud for sheer joy, and said, "I can do anything! I can do everything!"

"Your achievement is limited only by your imagination," said the old man. "I would warn you, though, against being overimaginative. Such a performance as this, before the wrong audience, might bring you to the stake. I once had a follower, a woman named Bertta, who was accused of witchcraft for her trick with the scarf and the ring. A simple sleight, nothing magical about it, yet she narrowly escaped death. It is wiser to reserve your greatest feats for select groups."

Beran turned on him angrily. "Why do you give me a gift and then warn me against it?"

"I promised that I would allow you fifty years, and I will keep my promise. But if you insist on throwing away your life by imprudence, I must come for you sooner."

"What do you mean?"

"If you intend to enjoy your gift and the rewards it will bring you, follow the advice you tried without success to give to your companion. Do not excel too greatly."

Beran frowned. He did not see how Sejourne's error applied to him. No one could accuse him of cheating or dishonesty; they would only marvel at his skill. He squatted down before the old man. "If I have the ability, why not use it to the full?"

The old man closed his eyes and pursed his lips thoughtfully, pressing his fingertips to his temple. At last, without opening his eyes, he said, "To be always slightly better than the rest is sufficient. You must not be so much better that they lose all hope of equaling you. It is permissible from time to time to allow yourself a moment of surpassing greatness, to astonish all who see you and leave them marveling for years to come. But such moments, by their very nature, must be rare. To place yourself beyond the reach and even the aspiration of all will arouse suspicion and envy. Those who might have admired you will find reason to speak against you. Accusations will follow. And where the people are ready to accuse, proof is easily found."

Beran shook his head slowly, his expression bleak. "Then what have I gained?"

The old man looked at him and smiled. "From now

on, you must perform only for kings and princes. They expect to be astonished, and need to be overawed."

"And how am I to meet—" Beran began, but the old man was gone without a sound, without so much as a tremor in the air.

6

The
Master

Beran followed the old man's advice—
which, after all, was no more than
his own advice to Sejourne, un-
heeded at a drastic price. He spent
the summer traveling from fair to fair, always pleasing
the crowds with feats they had never seen before, but
never with the marvelous or the impossible, which he
reserved for the proper audience. He took a quiet
amusement in hearing the people's cries of astonishment at some simple feat and knowing that he could
do things a hundred times more wonderful if he
pleased, and only their own limitations kept them
from seeing his full power.

It took him some time to accept the fact that nothing had changed but his skill. He looked no different.
He had half expected people to shrink from him in
horror, cross themselves and run from his path, but

everyone seemed to see him just as they had before. He bore no mark, gave off no whiff of brimstone as he passed, caused no fires to burn blue or dogs to howl. The church bells did not toll of their own accord when he walked by. After the first few weeks he realized that he felt no different than he always had. He had not become a monster, or a demon; he felt no desire to lead the innocent into evil ways, or do harm to all he met. He had simply made a pact, as many before him were known to have done, no more and no less. By summer's end, he was quite comfortable with himself, and thought little of the price he had pledged. Fifty years hence was too remote a time to worry about.

His takings were good, and now there was no partner to share them and no master to scoop up the greater part and toss him a few pennies. He was his own master. He bought himself a horse and, now that he no longer had to walk, a fine pair of boots, a cloak, and a splendid suit of clothes. He ate well and learned to speak knowingly about food and wines. He traveled alone, but he was never lonely. He could gather an appreciative audience at any alehouse or tavern, and talk his way around any woman he wanted. The women of the farms and villages were swayed by his glibness; they found his tales exciting, and his flattery comforting; those of the inn and tavern liked his effrontery, which matched their own. Beran's life was a festival, better than it had ever been, and this, he knew, was only the beginning.

Gian—or whatever he now called himself—had impressed him with his notion that a man might put a name on and take it off to suit his whim as casually as he would a cap or a cloak. He decided to adopt a fitting new name. "Beran" might serve for a village boy or an apprentice, but it was too simple for the grand person he had become. He recalled the names that had dropped so smoothly from the glib tongue of his old master, names of cold northern castles, ancient cities of the east, sun-flooded valleys in the south that flowed from the tongue like a song, and he recited them to himself with delight, comparing sounds as an artist mixes colors. From time to time he thought about Gian and wondered if he had met the fate of Sejourne, or the old juggler, or others he had heard about, some slain by robbers, others in tavern brawls, some found starved or frozen by the roadside in winter, prey to hunger, cold, and sickness. That, he knew, would not be his fate unless he acted foolishly. The old man had promised fifty years, and the old man kept his promises.

He traveled with no specific goal, for as yet his plans were indefinite. As Gian had done, he listened to the gossip of inn and alehouse, alert for the names of families known for their largesse and their delight in feats of skill and conjuring. His design was to become part of a great household and from there to work his way upward until he was called—as inevitably he would be—to serve the king. This, he knew, would come in time. For the present, he wanted only to be settled in comfort before winter came.

Near the end of summer, he met two men he had known during his days with Gian. They were minstrels, part of a troupe on their way to entertain at the wedding of the only daughter of a powerful knight. They did not recognize Beran at first in his finery, but when they had drunk a bit more ale, and he had recalled a few of their escapades and sung the older one's favorite ballad, they embraced him as a long-lost friend.

Beran's voice had deepened and grown stronger, and he had learned many new songs. Few of them were suited to a wedding, but they were popular in the tavern, and the night was merry. Before they parted, the minstrels had invited Beran to join them, and he had accepted.

"I call myself Berandolo. Berandolo of Benevento," he said.

The younger one laughed at this grandiose name. The older smiled and bowed with a mocking flourish. "And how long has that been your name?" he asked.

"Why should a man be satisfied with one name any more than he's satisfied with one boot?" said Beran. "Benevento is a great city in a land of surgeons and philosophers."

"And charlatans," said the younger minstrel.

"And musicians," Beran countered.

The other clapped him on the shoulder. "Call your-self what you will, you have a good voice and you're a good juggler, too."

"Did you see me today?"

"No, but I heard the people talking. Many of them said that they had never seen better, and never ex-pected to."

"I've learned a few things, and I practice every day," Beran said. He would say no more. Among the things he had learned was that it is far more effective to show one's ability than to boast of it. The others would see soon enough what he could do.

On the way to the castle of the knight, they stopped at several fairs and markets, and Beran gave his com-panions glimpses of his skill. He let them see enough to impress them, but he meant to save his best for the wedding festivities.

They arrived on a crisp autumn day, and that night they sang and played for the knight, a tall, imposing figure of a man named Hubert, and his household. When Beran's turn came, he juggled rings and torches in a dazzling display that had all in the hall cheering him. The next day, he begged audience with Sir Hubert. The knight received him, and was surprised when Beran proposed not a favor for himself but a feat to be performed before the bride and groom. The knight, who doted on his daughter, was enthusiastic at the suggestion and promised his full cooperation. It was to be a secret between him and Beran. They met often thereafter to discuss the plan and refine the details.

The wedding day was clear and bright, just cool enough for comfort. Bride and groom were dressed in their grandest garments, their silks and velvet trimmed with fur and fine lace, their boots of the softest leather worked with gold. Crowds lined the way to the church, as much to hear the music of the jongleurs as to cheer the young couple. After the nuptial Mass and the generous distribution of alms to the poor, the procession retraced its way, led by the musicians, to Sir Hubert's household. Then followed the wedding feast. Course after course came hot from the kitchen, fish and fowl, roast meats and pastries and sweets, soups and savories in great plenty, and, after them, the fruits and spiced wines and confections. Wine was abundant and of the finest. The minstrels played and sang, contortionists and tumblers went through their antics, the guests danced and sang carols, but Beran kept apart until well into the day. Then, at a sign from his host, he entered the hall.

By this time many of the company were in high spirits, and between the bustling of servants and the noise of guests and musicians, the hall was as clamorous as a marketplace. Beran entered amid this uproar.

His appearance attracted some attention, but did not silence the merrymakers. He wore tight-fitting garments of red and white, and high white boots. On his head was a broad-brimmed white hat with a scarlet plume. Behind him marched a servant, soberly attired, bearing in each hand a silver bowl.

Beran raised one hand, displaying three small pith balls between his fingers. He tossed two of the balls into the air and kept them up with his breath. The third joined them, all dancing rhythmically above the juggler's upturned face. The uproar in the hall diminished noticeably. Beran extended his other hand to reveal three more balls, and one by one he tossed them up to join the first three. He stood in a nonchalant pose, his hands on his hips, head bobbing under the floating pith balls, until all the hall was still. One great breath and all six balls flew high, only to be caught between his fingers, just as he had first displayed them.

Now that he had their attention, he was ready to astonish them. He beckoned to the servant, who stepped smartly to his side and held out the silver bowls. Beran took them and displayed them to the guests. One bowl contained eggs; the other was empty. He stopped before the bridal table, placed the bowls on two stools, swept off his hat, and bowed low. All this time he remained silent. His movements were graceful as a dancer's, his gestures slow and deliberate. The hall was hushed and attentive.

Still without a word, he turned his hat upside down and then inside out, displaying it to all before setting it on the floor before him. He then took the eggs from the bowl one by one, broke them into the hat, and dropped the empty shells into the other bowl. When he had broken all twelve eggs into the hat, he took it up gingerly amid subdued, expectant laughter and carried it to the table, where he crumbled a bit of bread into it, added honey and wine, and stirred the mixture with exaggerated gestures. He raised the hat high over his head, then quickly brought it down and turned it up-side down, and as half the onlookers gasped and the rest cried out in surprise, he snatched it up to reveal a steaming cake, which he presented to the bride with a courtly bow.

While laughter filled the hall, and some pounded their palms on the table to show their approval, he took up the bowl of crushed shells and drew from it three unbroken eggs, which he began to juggle. The servant tossed him additional eggs one by one until twelve were in the air. As they whirled before him, he kicked one of the bowls into the air, caught it on the toe of his boot, and balanced it there, then let the eggs fall into it one by one. When the last egg had fallen, he kicked the bowl into the air and caught it on his fingertips.

He took the unbroken eggs from the basket, six in each hand, and held them out to the bride. "My lady

Margery," he said in a clear voice that reached all corners of the hall, "I offer you a present from Sir Hubert of Vadoc, most loving of fathers and most generous of men. But it is not a gift of eggs or eggshells, my lady. He sends his beloved daughter a treasure far more precious." At the final word, he brought his hands together swiftly, crushing the shells between them. The shards fell away and he held a necklace of twelve flawless pearls, each of them the size of a cherry, strung on a gold chain. Beran raised it aloft, circling the hall to display it to all, at last laying it before the bride. With a bow to the bride and groom, and to Sir Hubert, he left the hall.

The next day, as the minstrels were preparing to leave, Beran was summoned to Sir Hubert's presence. The knight greeted him with a smile and, laying a hand on his shoulder in a fatherly way, led him to a window overlooking his fields.

"You have pleased me greatly, Berandolo. You have added to my daughter's happiness and delighted my guests," he said.

"You honor me to say so, Sir Hubert."

"I say no more than the truth. And I mean to reward you with more than words," said the knight, pressing two gold pieces into Beran's hand. Silencing his thanks with a gesture and a shake of the head, he went on, "Where do you and your companions go?"

"I will make my way south, to the sea. For the others, I know nothing of their plans."

"Do you not travel together, then?"

"No, my lord. They are old friends whom I happened to meet on the road. They asked me to join them, and I am grateful for that, but I prefer to work alone."

"The world is a hard place for a man alone. Would it not be better to belong to a household where you would be sure of shelter and food and companions?"

"It would indeed, my lord. But I am not a warrior or a priest. I cannot read, nor heal, nor handle animals, nor make things grow. I have only the skill you saw."

"It is a skill I value. I have no sons and only one daughter, the image of her mother, may she rest in peace," said Sir Hubert, crossing himself. "My daughter is leaving me now, and the winter is coming. This castle will be a silent, gloomy place. You will help to brighten the dark days."

"I am honored to serve you, my lord," said Beran, bowing.

"And I am pleased to have you, Berandolo. The steward will acquaint you with the routine of the castle, and assign you a place to sleep. You may say your farewells to your friends now, if you like."

Beran left him with a light heart. Things were turning out as he had hoped, and in good time. Visitors would be arriving for the hunting season, and some of them, at least, would merit a feast and entertainment. Word of his skill would spread. When Sir Hubert was summoned to his overlord, or the overlord visited, anticipation would already be aroused. The next step on Beran's way would be smoother.

The steward, a dour, gray man named Gabriel, took Beran to a chamber containing a narrow bed and a chest. His words were courteous, his manner distant. His disapproval of such fine accommodations for a mere juggler was plain from his expression.

Beran showed equal courtesy, though he cared little for the steward's opinion. He knew how to make friends, and which friends were worth making.

He got on well with all in the castle, from stable boys to kitchen staff. His readiness to perform some simple feat, to juggle horseshoes or turnips, milking stools or drinking vessels or anything else that might be at hand, to sing a love song or compose an impromptu comic ballad to mark some household incident, quickly made him welcome everywhere. Even the steward paused in his rounds to watch him, and bestowed a grudging nod of approbation. Beran never wanted for an attentive and appreciative audience. He never lacked food and drink and companionship, be it the raucous fellowship of men or the gentler company of women.

Sometimes, when the day was clear and the sun full, he took all his traps and went off by himself, riding far from the castle to a secluded spot where he might exercise his talent to the full without the danger of jealous or suspicious watchers. He amused himself with the thought of someday displaying his ability unchecked to the world, savoring the imagined cries of awe and wonder and terror in the presence of the marvelous. But for now he would have to be content with an audience of himself and the woodland creatures who crept to the edges of the clearing to observe this man who came into their world not to hunt and kill, but to make objects dance in the air at his command.

Sir Hubert was a devout man who began each day with Mass in his chapel, a small chamber within the castle. As a member of the household, Beran was obliged to attend. On the first day, he passed through the chapel doors with an unaccustomed sensation of anxiety, uncertain of what might befall. Would God permit a man to kneel before Him in worshipful show when that man had pledged himself to the eternal enemy? Might he not be risking destruction and damnation on the spot if he dared enter, and kneel, and cross himself?

Beran did not doubt that God was real, and present, and aware of everything that he had done. If God did not exist, then the other could not exist, either, and he knew that the other was real. He told himself that God was too busy with the affairs of emperors and kings, with steering the stars and the planets and governing the seas and the weather, to bother with a juggler. Nonetheless he was uncomfortable. When the first morning passed without a bolt from the heavens, he breathed more easily. From then on, he attended Mass with as much outward piety as Sir Hubert himself.

He became friendly with one of the steward's men, a clerk named Albert who had been educated by the monks. Albert was able to read and write Latin, knew some Greek, and could calculate with numbers. He was a few years older than Beran, and learned in speech; but having spent all his life within walls of one sort or another, he was innocent as a child in the ways of the world.

While Beran was no more than mildly impressed by Albert's scholarship, Albert was completely overawed by Beran's skill and his easy self-confidence. He was so shy that they might never have spoken had Beran not taken the initiative, but once his reserve was broken down, the scholar became Beran's inseparable companion. Beran's stories of his adventures, some of them imaginary and all of them embellished, held him spellbound. Beran's songs often made him blush and duck his head guiltily, but he learned many of them by heart.

One day, as they walked in the orchard, Albert said, "Will you teach me to juggle?"

"If you like. But why do you want to learn? What good will juggling do you when you're a steward?"

Albert frowned and said in a petulant voice, "Perhaps I shall not be a steward. It would be pleasant to be a wayfarer, and see the world."

"A wayfarer's life is not easy, Albert."

"That matters little to me. I have no wish to grow old and die here in this castle."

Beran stopped and took him by the shoulders. "Listen to me, my friend. The world is a dangerous place. I can teach you to juggle, and to do other tricks, but that won't make the world any safer. You've seen how good I am—"

"The best we have ever seen," Albert broke in.

"Well, good as I am, I've been cold and hungry. There were times I thought I'd starve. I've had to fight for my life. I've done things that you could never do."

"I still wish to learn to juggle as you do. I know I can never be as good as you are, and perhaps I will never have the courage to leave my place here, but I must try."

Beran shrugged. "Very well, I'll teach you."

"And in return, I will teach you to read and write, and to calculate with numbers."

"You needn't repay me, Albert."

"Oh, but I want to. It is good to know such things."

"What good are reading and writing and numbers to me?"

"You will be able to keep accounts. You will be a

rich man one day, and you will always be able to know how much you have."

Beran laughed. "If I'm rich, I'll have a steward to do it for me."

"It is best not to depend too much on others. And you should learn to read. You like to tell stories, and when you can read, you can learn the stories others have told."

Beran considered Albert's offer. The castle was a dull place in midwinter. He had plenty of idle time during the short, gloomy days and often in the evenings as well, and he was curious about those rows of black marks that Albert and others found meaningful while to him they were no more than lines and circles. Perhaps they could tell him something.

"It might even save your life one day," Albert said.

"Indeed? And how can reading save me from anything?" Beran said, smiling. The very thought seemed ridiculous.

"If you should be taken for a crime, and you can read, you have the right to be tried in an ecclesiastical court. That could save your life."

Here was the most persuasive argument of all, and it tipped the balance. "All right, then, Albert," Beran said. "I'll teach you to juggle, and you can teach me to read."

They were to begin the next day, but in the morning

Beran had a mishap that left him unable to juggle for nearly a week. It occurred in the kitchen, where he often visited. The comfort of his present situation had not erased his memories of hunger and cold and want, and he was pleased to know that for a trifling feat, or a song, or a joke, he could eat and drink his fill before a great fire whenever he pleased.

On this morning, Beran noticed several small copper bowls and a pitcher of milk on the worktable when he entered. He promised the cook and his staff a feat they would never see duplicated. He had a kitchen maid fill three bowls brimful with milk. He set one on top of his head, took up the other two, and announced that he would juggle all three without spilling a drop.

The cook, who always scoffed before Beran attempted a feat and then cheered the loudest when he brought it off, said, "Do this, and you'll have a bowl of good fat soup with a chunk of meat in it, and all the bread you wish. I'll serve you myself."

"Done. And make sure it's a big bowl. And a clean one."

Beran began, and the cook and maids and kitchen boys gasped at the sight of the three bowls crossing before him without spilling their contents. Beran spun around on one toe, crossed his hands, and balanced on a stool that he tilted until it stood on one leg, and all the while not a drop was lost.

One of the kitchen boys, Cuddy, a simple lad not

much more than a halfwit, was greatly excited by the show. He clapped and shouted, and in his unthinking enthusiasm to become a part of the excitement, he took up with the tongs a copper cup that had been standing near the fire and was searing hot. "Here, master, here!" he shouted, tossing it to Beran.

Beran caught it without thinking, and at once cried out in pain. The bowls clattered to the flags and milk splashed and spattered everywhere. As Beran grimaced and wrung his hand, the cook seized Cuddy and beat him until blood ran, then flung him to the floor.

"Now clean up the mess you've made, you idiot, and do it right or I'll beat you again!" he cried, shaking his fist at the wailing boy.

"He's had enough," Beran said. "The poor fool meant no harm."

"But he did harm. What if the master calls for you tonight?"

"Then I'll be uncomfortable. I'll need that bowl of soup to keep my strength up."

"You shall have it," said the cook, signaling urgently to one of the kitchen boys. He placed the bowl before Beran with his own hands, and set a fresh loaf and butter beside it. He was very much afraid, for he knew that Beran was a favorite of Sir Hubert's.

The burn was not serious, and Beran said nothing of the incident to anyone outside the kitchen, but it gave him matter for thought. Whatever else his compact with the old man involved, it did not confer any kind of immunity or protection. His hand was vulnerable, and he could be forced into clumsiness by a foolish or malicious act. The old man had intimated as much, and now it was made plain.

Beran and Albert began working together three days later, by which time Albert was fidgeting with impatience. He was an earnest but clumsy pupil, and it was weeks before he could keep three soft cloth balls in the air even for a very brief time, but once he had done so, he was exultant. He began to talk as if he were ready to begin his travels. Beran had to dampen his enthusiasm with the warning that no one would stop to watch him, much less reward him, until he could do considerably more than juggle three balls. It was no easier to become a master juggler than to become a scholar; years of work lay ahead.

In truth, Beran was uncomfortable at the thought of Albert, with his pallid hands and face, and his clerkish ways, trying to survive in the world beyond the castle. He felt no obligation to dissuade him. He doubted that Albert would ever choose to leave his comfortable life here, but he did not want to leave him unprepared and full of illusions.

Beran's own progress was slow. He quickly mastered numbers, and took pleasure in working simple calculations. Letters were much more difficult. He learned their names, but having done so, he still stared at the marks until they crawled before his eyes like ants, and could make no sense of them. Pride made him persist, and Albert was a patient teacher. Gradually Beran began to put the letters together, and then to recognize words, and at last to extract meaning from them. And having done so, he lost interest, for the books Albert showed him all told of saints and holy living.

"Where are all the good stories?" he asked, disappointed.

"We don't have any books like that in the castle. Father Martin has these, and a Bible and a commentary. He might let you look at his Bible someday. That has good stories in it."

"Father Martin doesn't like me very much. I can tell from the way he always looks at me when he talks about sinners."

"I'll talk to him. Once he gets to know you, he'll be generous," Albert said.

Beran no longer cared. He could read enough to save his neck. Spring was coming, and there would be better things to do than huddle before a fire in the castle and struggle to make sense out of squiggles on a page.

Before Beran could win the chaplain's confidence, Sir Hubert began preparations for a visit to his overlord, Merabon of Viers. As a subtenant, albeit a powerful one, he owed his lord a period of service. He was to leave with a small party some three weeks hence.

Gabriel, the steward, brought the news that Beran was to be a member of the party. He was as dour as ever, but even his solemn mien could not conceal his excitement. "You are a most fortunate young man," he told Beran. "Never before has Sir Hubert taken a minstrel, or a juggler, or any such person with him. He thinks highly of you, and believes that you will please the lord Merabon."

"I'll not merely please him, Gabriel, I'll astonish him."

The steward frowned. "Do not be proud. Lord Merabon has traveled far and seen much. He has been to the Holy Land, and fought the pagans in the north and the Moors across the Great Sea."

"He's traveled farther than I, but I'll still show him feats he's never seen before. Sir Hubert will not regret his decision, Gabriel."

Shaking his head and muttering about youth and vanity, the steward left him. Once alone, Beran sprang into the air, did a sprightly little dance, and clapped his hands for joy. All was going as he had hoped. Laughing softly to himself, he began to plan his performance.

7

The
Friar

The forest in early spring was a delight to the senses and a boon to the spirit. The roads were muddy, the going slow and tedious, but after a winter's confinement in the dark and odorous castle, the journey was like an escape. Birds sang from dawn till dark, the scent of fresh new life pervaded the moist air, and all around them, under the bright pale skies, the woods glowed in a thousand shades of green.

The castle of Lord Merabon crouched on the crest of a hill at the top of a long rise, commanding a clear view in all directions. It was first visible while they were hours away, and loomed ever larger and more imposing as they drew near. Compared with Sir Hubert's castle, it was like a cathedral to a roadside chapel. From without, it appeared impregnable behind its broad moat and many-towered walls, a stronghold defended by nature and the work of man. Once they had passed through the gates, it became a bustling, crowded village.

The yard was as full, and as busy, as a marketplace. Men and women came and went through doorways, hurried in and out of sheds and storage buildings carrying bundles and baskets, leading horses, shouting orders, directing servants of the great lords' guests. Other knights had arrived shortly before their party, and a small knot of them stood together, talking and laughing loudly. Sir Hubert left his entourage to join them.

Beran observed his surroundings with increasing delight. Here was a proper place to display his skill, an audience to appreciate and reward him and spread word of his gifts.

Since the marriage of his daughter, Sir Hubert's castle had been without a woman's presence. The visitors were all fellow knights or tenants of small consequence. Knights, Beran had quickly learned, were men of action. They cared little for subtlety or refinement. Their respect was for courage, strength, and mastery of a difficult skill. For them, the mere fact that he kept one more ball or plate in the air than the last juggler they had seen was enough to win their approval. When he added the risk of daggers or torches, they applauded all the louder. But they grew bored at any display of finesse. They would not have cared to see him juggle vessels of liquid without spilling the contents unless the vessels contained boiling oil or corrosive poisons. In that case, they would have shouted his praises if he succeeded, and delighted all the more in a mishap.

But at Viers things would be different. Lord Merabon had a wife and two daughters, as well as two sons, and the women were well attended. Beran would have opportunities to show all facets of his talent to those who could appreciate what they were seeing.

That very night there was a feast, and he gave the company a sample of his talent. He had learned from Sejourne the trick of addressing his equipment as if it were alive, and from Gian the effectiveness of glib patter in attracting and holding a crowd's attention. He combined the two, keeping up a kind of commentary to which his audience were drawn in as privileged confidantes, as if they were privy to his thoughts.

As he sent his daggers flashing aloft, he referred to them by name, as if they were partners each playing a role of his or her own. "There you go, Will, and you, too, Jeanne, yes, and now you, Alouette, that's right, that's the way you must behave, very nice, very nice indeed. Oh, they're good, these three, they know what to do and they do it nicely, no arguments from them, no tricks, no surprises for their old friend Berandolo. There you go, nice and smooth, and now it's time for a friend to join you," he said, adding a fourth dagger. "Here's your old friend Leon, you're glad to see him, aren't you? Of course you are, look at the way you greet him and fit him in so nicely, you all work so well together, everyone helping, no one getting out of place or causing trouble, just old friends out for a dance together, showing what you can do, making everyone happy, that's how we do it, we want to do our best and see everyone smile and hear them cheer us on, don't we? Of course we do, my friends, and so we'll ask a few more old companions to join us." Two more daggers joined the four, and he said, "Now you must be firm with these two, but patient also, for they are twins, but no more alike than wool and iron. This fellow Guy is a shifty one, you must keep an eye on him, he's full of sly tricks and he'll cut you if he can, but his brother is a fine decent fellow, a good influence if only Guy would listen to him and follow his example. You must all do your best to keep him honest." Two more daggers would join the six, and be described to the onlookers as if they were pupils being presented by a stern schoolmaster, and then two more, and two more, until twelve daggers were describing a silver arc before him. Beran might have added a dozen more, but he knew that he was already doing more than anyone had ever done before him, and need do no more on his first night here. He made his way slowly backward, to where a table had been set up by one of the servants, and twelve rings laid out on the tabletop. Sending the daggers higher and higher and then bidding a final farewell to his friends, addressing each by name, Beran let them fall behind him one by one. Each landed precisely in the center of a ring.

When he next performed, Beran offered something quite different. With the help of a forester, he cut and peeled six wands, each of them as tall as he and thick as his thumb, and decorated them with bright stripes. After juggling them long enough to arouse everyone's anticipation, he stopped and then stood one on his palm. One by one, he tossed the rest aloft and caught them end to end, until they towered in a slender column halfway to the roof of the great hall. At his signal, a servant tossed a platter high in the air. Beran caught it and balanced it on the very top of the column, set it spinning, and then, with a flip of his hand, stood it on edge still slowly spinning. As the company in the hall shouted their approval, he had the servant toss up Lord Merabon's empty goblet, which he caught and balanced atop the platter, and then a cluster of grapes, which he caught in the goblet. With a shout, he flung up his hands and the whole edifice shuddered and collapsed. Too quickly for the eye to follow, he caught the wands in a neat bundle, the platter, still spinning, atop the bundle, and the goblet in his other hand. The grapes had vanished. Raising the goblet to his lips, Beran sipped and then set the goblet, nearly brimful of wine, before Lord Merabon.

For the climax, he performed a variation on the feat

that had won him favor from Sir Hubert. He began with twelve silver rings. When all twelve were in the air, he made a slow circuit of the hall and stopped before the lady Anne, wife of Lord Merabon. Dropping to one knee, he caught the rings and then, with a flourish, spun them around in his hands and flung out his arms to display not twelve but thirteen rings linked in a chain. Twelve of the rings were silver; the central ring was bright green. Bringing his hands together, he asked the lady Anne to lay her napkin over them. When she had done so, he raised his hands high, shook off the napkin, and opened them to reveal a delicate silver chain from which depended a single emerald. He took up the napkin, laid the necklace on it, and presented it to the lady Anne while Merabon, beside her, looked on beaming with pride.

From that time on, Beran could not go anywhere in the castle without being pressed for a display of his skill. He was always cheerful, obliging to all, disappointed no one, and left the castle buzzing with his name. He knew perfectly well that the knights had assembled for business, not amusement, and that the advancement and rewarding of a juggler had no place in their thoughts; but he knew too that to please the company would please Lord Merabon, and the favor of a powerful magnate could take him far.

He brought himself to Merabon's particular attention one rainy day. It was the fifth consecutive day of rain in a chill and gloomy week. Deprived of the hunting they enjoyed second only to battle, the knights were in a temper as dark and foul as the weather. Horses and hounds were restless, the falcons wanted exercise, and the men were edgy. Tempers were short. Such words as were exchanged were few and harsh, and more than once hands went to sword hilts at some trivial remark.

Beran was present when two knights exchanged bitter words and swords were drawn and ready for combat. Guards parted and disarmed them, but the air was hot with anger. Friends of the two gathered, and Merabon's men found themselves outnumbered and threatened. Beran sensed an opportunity.

He strolled up to the knot of angry men and asked the guards if he might hold the swords taken from the two knights. He hefted them, tossed them end over end, and asked two of the other knights to lend him theirs. They complied, as much out of curiosity as trust. He began to juggle the four blades, and more than once even these hardened men had their hearts in their mouths at the narrow margin of steel and flesh. He balanced a pair in each hand, pommel to pommel, the points to his palm, then flung them high and resumed juggling, making his way out the gate into the yard. Those in the hall followed and a greater crowd gathered, knights and men-at-arms, armorers and stable boys and kitchen maids, and Beran, chatting away all the while in a casual conversation with blades and onlookers, added first a stool, then a bucket, a measuring scoop, and a broom to the blades dancing at his direction.

His words grew livelier, and the onlookers began to laugh at the gibes he directed at the obedient objects and at them. Even the two knights who had first quarreled could not hold back a smile as Beran compared swords to bucket and broom and other undignified implements of labor, all of them much the same when whirling through the air at the hands of a juggler. He kept up his show until he saw Lord Merabon and six of his men approaching; then he brought it to a dramatic climax. He caught the stool with his foot and set it down, keeping all the rest in the air. Then he caught the bucket, placing it between his feet, and then the broom and scoop, standing them in the bucket. Finally he seated himself on the stool, sent the four blades high into the air, and let them sink point first into the ground on all four sides of him no more than a finger's breadth away while he sat coolly with his arms folded, one foot on the rim of the bucket.

The crowd quenched their enthusiasm and quickly dispersed at Lord Merabon's arrival, and Beran, too, took his leave. But later that day he was summoned to the great lord's presence.

"You have acted bravely, juggler," the knight said without preamble, "And you deserve a reward."

"I did what seemed needful, my lord."

"You might have been gutted for it. This weather has everyone in a foul temper."

"I was sure your lordship's men would protect me."

Merabon laughed sharply. "You have more faith in them than I do. They let themselves be cowed, and you saved the day. I want to keep you here for a time."

"You honor me, my lord."

"You've earned a place. I never had much use for tumblers and minstrels and that lot, still don't, but you're better than the rest of them, young as you are. Every one I've ever seen would have run away today, but you put your skill to good use." The knight raised a monitory hand. "Don't thank me again. One of the steward's men will show you your place. Here, take this," he said, tossing Beran a gold coin.

Beran felt no pang at the thought of leaving Sir Hubert so abruptly. Each of them did as he was commanded, and an overlord's wishes were not to be denied.

For two years and more Beran, as Berandolo of Benevento, served Merabon to his lord's pleasure and his own advantage. Visitors marveled at the juggler's skill, and each new arrival was shown something new and even more amazing than anything he or she expected. The men saw displays of courage and daring, the women feats of elegant skill, and all were treated to moments of wonder bordering on magic. Beran seldom repeated himself and never disappointed.

Still, he found it necessary to go off alone from time to time and give his ability free rein. To have done so before a single witness would, he knew, place him under suspicion of sorcery; but to deny himself the full exercise of his powers for too long a time was a kind of choking that he could not endure.

Lord Merabon's household attended Mass every morning, but with considerably less piety than had been shown by Sir Hubert and his people. It was customary for Merabon to hold discussions and to have documents read to him during the ceremony, and he often left in the middle of a sermon or at other equally inopportune moments. Beran followed the relaxed example of the others. He did not presume to come and go at will, but he absented himself in spirit, staring at the statues and the windows, planning new feats, and occasionally nodding off. He cared little for spiritual things, and went for long periods of time without giving a thought to his pact with the old man. Of the fifty promised years, fewer than five had passed. There would be ample time to worry later.

One morning a stranger appeared in the chapel. He was a friar, a gaunt man in threadbare black cloak and hood over a well-worn white tunic. He assisted the chaplain at Mass, and when the sermon came, it was the friar who ascended into the pulpit.

No one slept through the sermon on this day, or ogled a neighbor, or dreamed of the hunt. The man had a voice like a clarion and a message that chilled the blood of the most hardened listener. He spoke of temptation and the need for vigilance and resolution to resist it, of sin and the necessity of repentance and atonement, of damnation and eternal pain and sorrow and loss. His eyes seemed to fix on each of his listeners, to penetrate their souls and bring light flooding in upon their darkest and most shameful secrets.

Beran listened in growing dread. The armor of careless confidence that he had erected around himself over the years crumpled like an eggshell under a boot. The friar's message was all too clear. He had been found out. The man was speaking to him. The words might be heard by all present, but the message was addressed to Beran and to him alone. The friar knew of his pact and had come to reveal it and condemn him, to make a terrible example of him before Merabon and his household.

He dared not look up at the man perched above them, leaning forward, darting his glance from side to side, seeming to accuse all with his gaze and spare none from his warning, though it was meant for one man among them only. The friar spoke on for what seemed hours to Beran, and his words rang in Beran's ears long after he had descended from the pulpit and rejoined the priest at the altar.

Beran left the chapel trembling. His secret had not been revealed, but he felt no relief. He overheard a knight laugh and turn to his companion with the common gibe, "He is a friar, therefore a liar," but he found no cause for amusement in the words, and no consolation. The friar knew, as clearly as if he had been in the forest on that day. He had seen into Beran's soul, and he knew.

Beran paced through the castle, keeping to the places where he would have people around him, and noise, and distracting activity. He did not want to be alone to brood on the friar's words, and on his fate.

He went eventually to the kitchen and took some bread and milk, finding slight comfort in the routine comings and goings of the kitchen staff. But he had no appetite for food, and was too restless to remain long. He wandered out to the yard, and there he saw the friar surrounded by a ring of stable boys who listened to his words as if entranced.

Beran had no desire to see or hear the friar again, only to be far from him, but some perverse impulse drew him to the edge of the little circle. The boys were squatting in the dirt, or hunkered down. Only he and the friar remained standing.

The friar's manner was different now. Preaching to youths in the open air, under the bright morning sun, he spoke in a gentle voice, earnest as a father urging his children. "Matthew has given us the message of our Lord. It is a hard message, but we must heed it if we are to be saved. The message is simple. Nothing is to be cherished above God, nothing is more important than salvation. Nothing, however precious to us! If your eyes lead you into sin, pluck them out. Tear them from your head," he said with a sudden dramatic gesture, as if he were indeed pulling out his own eyes. One of the boys cried out in horror, and others gasped. The friar stood with bowed head, clawed hands before his eyes; then he looked up and his gaze fixed on Beran. He took a few quick strides closer and shot out a hand to seize Beran's right wrist. "If your hand leads you astray, or your foot, then strike it off. What use is hand or foot or eye amid the fires of hell? Better far to leave this life blind or maimed and enter His presence, where all will be made well, than to burn whole and entire for all eternity!"

The friar's eyes shone as he spoke these words, and Beran remembered the look in the eyes of Gilbert of Sanlac when he spoke of the miracle he anticipated. He jerked his wrist free and staggered backward, raising his other hand as if to shield himself from that gaze. Then he turned and ran from the yard.

In his tiny chamber he looked down at his right hand. The red mark in his palm now looked swollen and hideous to him, like some blasphemous parody of the stigmata. He drew his dagger and pressed the point against the spot in his palm, but he could not go further. He let the dagger fall and sank to the floor, whimpering. He knew what he must do, but he lacked the courage. He feared the revelation of his foul state, he feared hell, he feared the friar, he feared the old man, he feared pain and want and hunger, and his fears left him paralyzed. He was beyond repentance. He had sold himself to the enemy of God and man. No suffering possible on or beyond this earth could ever atone for what he had done. Others might hope, but not he. He was lost.

He lay for a time limp and helpless, and then, in a feverish flurry of activity, he rolled his clothing in a blanket, took up the chest of his traps, and returned to the yard, taking the way that led him directly to the stables. No one questioned him. They were accustomed to seeing him ride out from time to time with all his juggling gear, and even his distracted manner on this day did not arouse their curiosity.

He rode for hours without stopping, and only when he had stopped was he aware of his hunger. He had brought no food, and no inn was near. He had to satisfy himself and his exhausted horse with water from a brook.

He rested for a time, and changed into a plain outfit and sturdy hunting boots. He started to roll up his castle finery, for it would bring a good price. But he flung it from him in a sudden rage, connecting it with the folly that had led to his damnation. Let it rot here in the woods, and taint no other foolish soul.

He rode on aimlessly, sleeping wherever he found himself at nightfall, eating whatever came to hand. He had no destination. For long periods of time he was completely unaware of his surroundings, and he would become suddenly conscious of pelting rain, or bitter wind. The first weeks were painful, for life in the castle had softened him and made him unfit for the hard life of the road.

For a long time he did not juggle. He let his beard grow, but one day, in a flash of awareness, he shaved it off. He could easily disguise himself from men, but it was not men he fled. No disguise could deceive the power that pursued him. Flee where he might, hide where he would, the outcome was certain.

More than once he thought of hacking off the hand that damned him, forfeiting his pledge and freeing himself as the friar had said, but he always faltered when it came to the act. When he saw a beggar with a missing hand, he looked on him with envy and not pity, and wished that they could change places, for even the most wretched, maimed beggar had a hope that he had lost.

He was sparing with his money, but at last it was gone. Piece by piece he sold his possessions, and finally his horse, retaining only his juggling gear. He proceeded on foot, wandering from town to town, to fair and marketplace, and he began to juggle once again simply to stay alive.

His manner was different now. He did not speak, but worked in silence, abstracted, almost hostile, as if a disapproving onlooker to his own deeds. He was less cautious, and often left the crowd in awe and some slight fear. He had a vague hope that some wondrous feat might transgress the bounds of credibility and bring upon him the suspicions of the authorities, who would do what he was unable to do. One stroke of the axe, a moment of terrible pain, and then he might hope again. But there were no accusations, only the tinkle of coins, the empty and meaningless sounds of praise.

He wandered on in this way for three years, always alone, friendless and isolated even amid the noise and cheer of inn and tavern and campsite. No trace of his years of comfort and plenty now remained. His face was gaunt and weather-beaten, his clothes were threadbare, his boots cracked. Sometimes he remained a week or more in one spot, but more often he stayed only a single night. He seldom knew the name of the place he was in, or the place he had left. Such things did not matter anymore.

All places and roads were as one to him. His way took him east, then south, until he was far from the land of his birth and the rugged countryside he knew. In the early autumn he came to a valley where a walled city rose at the confluence of two rivers. The roads were empty, and the outlying settlements seemed mean and squalid places where a traveler would find only hostility. He followed the high road to the city and entered the gate unquestioned. Only when he came to the market square, and overheard merchants talking, did he learn that this was the domain of Count Osostro.

The name meant nothing to him. He laid his pack down and took out his daggers. Climbing to the top of a barrel, he began to juggle.

The
Misfortune
of
Count
Ososdro

ith the juggler's departure, the count Osostro seemed to recover his old assurance; but after several days he fell to brooding once more. On the tenth day, after a restless night, he gave order that the severed hand be dug from the rubbish heap and brought to the palace yard. At his command a huge fire was built and the bloated, discolored hand cast in. The count watched until it was consumed and the blackened bones pounded fine and scattered to the winds.

By midwinter a change had become obvious to everyone. The count had always been a cautious man; now he kept even his closest advisers and retainers at three paces' distance. He allowed no one to touch him. He shrank from a raindrop, the brush of a falling leaf, the touch of a snowflake. On a festival day, when a small child came up to him unseen and slipped her hand into his, he cried out in an awful voice, and collapsed on the spot. To the surprise of all who had witnessed the incident, the child and her family went unpunished.

From that day on, the count remained withindoors. His ways became ever more reclusive until, at the end, his world had shrunk to a small tower room bare of all furnishings but a simple plank bed and table. Only a single servant was allowed to enter, and when he did, the count withdrew to the farthest corner of the room and stood with drawn sword until the man had left. Torches burned in the chamber day and night, and two guards stood outside the door at all times.

The door remained closed, but unlocked. The guards heard the count moving about, talking to himself, sometimes shouting, though they could not distinguish words. Their orders were to remain outside unless expressly summoned, to let no one else enter but at the count's command, and they obeyed.

It was in the tower room that the count died. The guards heard him shriek in terror, and then cry out for help. Taking this cry as a command, they entered the room and found the count writhing on the floor, naked and smeared with blood. His clothing and the bedding were in shreds, and he was clawing wildly at his flesh, rending and tearing as if to rip away some unseen thing that crawled over him. He had torn strips of flesh from his stomach and chest, and gouged bloody furrows in his face. When the guards tried to restrain his hands, he screamed as if he had fallen into the clutches of fiends, and died shrieking in their grip.

It was given out that the count had died of a sudden fever, and no one questioned the story. He left no heir. The lord chamberlain and a council of nobles took command, and their rule was just. The people, from the beggars to the nobility, were much relieved.

No monument was built to the count Osostro, and the statues he had erected of himself were dismantled one by one until none remained. His name was seldom spoken. In a very few years, in the land he had once ruled, he was forgotten except for the tales told of him to frighten unruly children.

8

The
Artisan

Beran passed through the city gate and made his way south. Despite frequent applications of Count Osostro's ointment, the stump of his wrist still ached, and a careless touch would set it to throbbing. He often awoke at night to feel the missing fingers twitching and burning.

He accepted his pains without complaint; indeed, he embraced them with joy, for they were proof of his deliverance. Each day he blessed the name of Count Osostro, a name cursed by so many before him. His hand was gone, his pledge fulfilled, his bondage ended. The old man no longer had a claim on him. He was free.

And not only had the count rescued him from certain damnation, he had made him wealthy and given him protection. Beran was received with respect and

fear wherever he went, even far beyond the boundaries
of the count's lands. The haughty phrasing of his letter
proved most effective with all who read it. Those who
could not read beheld the seal and the flourishes of the
scribe's hand, and bowed to the authority of the bearer.
When Beran told his story, fear changed to wonder,
and respect grew. The count's cruelty was well
known, as was his capricious dispensing of justice, but
never before had such extremes of severity and generosity been joined.

At an inn near a mountain pass, a clean and comfortable place where he remained for most of the winter,
the innkeeper's young son listened hungrily to Beran's
tales of his old life. Andreas was a stocky boy, cheerful
as a puppy and as full of energy. He attached himself to
the juggler like a squire to his knight.

One crisp bright morning when the air was still, he
drew Beran aside and asked him to come to the stable.
There he took three soft cloth balls from a hiding place
and began to juggle. He was awkward in his movements, with little of the natural grace that made a
good juggler, but his face glowed with pleasure. Beran
watched, recalling the boy he had once been and the
enthusiasm with which he had first displayed his own
simple talent. He might have been as clumsy as Andreas; he did not remember. He remembered only his
cruel rebuff at the hands of one whose approval he
sought, and resolved to spare the boy that pain.

"Who taught you, Andreas?" he asked.

"I learned by myself. I saw a man at a fair, and I watched him closely and copied everything he did."

"That's how I learned too. You've done well."

"I want to be a juggler. I want to travel and see the places you've seen, and be part of a great household."

Beran laid his left hand gently on the boy's shoulder. "It's not always like that, Andreas. I haven't told you of the times I went without eating for three days running, or the times I had to walk all night long through snowdrifts above my knees because if I'd stopped even to catch my breath I'd have frozen to death. I've been hunted and attacked, beaten more than once, robbed. . . ." He held up the stump of his right hand. "I've even lost my hand. It's been a hard life, and I'm glad to have it behind me."

"But you were a great juggler!"

"I was very good. But the price was too high."

"I think you were the best. You must have been the best."

Beran laughed gently and repeated a remembered observation. "And if I were the best, how would I know? The world is a big place. Maybe when I thought I was doing a great feat there was someone in a distant land, a land I'll never see or know about, doing things that exceeded anything I could imagine. Be as good as you can be, Andreas, and don't worry about being the best."

"Will you teach me?"

"You've already taught yourself."

"But I don't know anything! You could show me all the things you've learned."

"There's little that can be taught. No one can teach the truly important things. You must learn them for yourself."

"Oh, Beran, please, please! I want so much to learn!"

The boy's eagerness conquered him. With a shrug he said, "Very well, Andreas. But only if your parents have no objection."

The boy's face fell. "My father beat me the first time he found me juggling. He said it was an idler's pastime." He put a hand to his mouth and looked up guiltily. Beran only laughed. The boy brightened at once and went on with great confidence. "But that was before he knew you. Now that he's talked to you, he'll feel differently. If you asked him, Beran, he'd permit it."

Beran broached the subject that evening. The innkeeper was a kindly man, but excessively conventional and armored in his prejudices. He was clearly uncomfortable with the offer. His wife shook her head dolefully, but would not refuse outright. Beran sensed that she was doing her best to reconcile her pleasure at his interest in the boy's ability with her fear of Andreas's being led into an idle life.

"Andreas has his work to do. He must not put anything before it," said the father.

"I could teach him in the evening, when the work was done."

"That is generous of you," said the mother.

"And only if everything was done to your satisfaction. If he left any work undone, there'd be no more lessons."

The father scratched his balding crown. This conversation was clearly one he wished over with. "You're a decent man, Master Beran, and I mean you no disrespect, but to speak plainly, I've met few jugglers or minstrels or people of that sort that I'd want in this house."

"I've met bad ones myself," Beran said, concealing his amusement behind a solemn face. "But it wasn't the juggling that made them bad. They'd have been wicked farmers, or blacksmiths, or even innkeepers. It's the man who does evil, not his talents."

"Ah, that's true," said the mother. "If the wickedness is in a man, it will come out."

"Your Andreas is a good lad. And knowing a few simple tricks would make him a better innkeeper. Think how pleasant it would be if he could entertain your guests of an evening."

The father's expression softened. "That's true. And it might make the boy work harder."

"I'm sure it would. And it would make the guests happier."

They agreed; and after exacting a few promises from the boy, Beran began instructing him in the evenings at the fireside. Oftentimes the boy's mother and father, pretending to work at some small chore, watched them covertly and exchanged silent satisfied glances. After the life of the road and the castle, Beran found this domesticity comforting. Andreas would never be capable of anything but the simplest feats, but he was so eager to learn that his work around the inn improved and his parents were delighted with both him and their guest.

When he departed, in the spring, Beran presented Andreas with all his juggler's traps and gear. To him they were useless baggage with unpleasant associations, and the boy could have been no more grateful to receive the rings and daggers and painted balls if they had been made of gold.

He thought sometimes of Andreas in the days that followed, and was almost envious of the boy. How fortunate, he reflected, to be blessed with a small gift. Too great ability can be a curse, creating a hunger that cannot be sated. He pictured Andreas in years to come taking delight in amusing friends and visitors with a simple feat of juggling, living out his days as a happy and successful innkeeper, telling his children how he had wrestled with the choice of life and finally rejected the great world to marry their mother and raise a proper family. They would listen, and watch him juggle three plates, and think him a great man. Andreas would live the life his parents had lived, and so would his children, and their children after them, and all would be very happy and comfortable with it. Beran saw in such a life attractions that he had not suspected. A few years earlier, the prospect would have seemed to him unbearably pinched and narrow, but now he looked at things with different eyes.

He spent the summer in search of an artisan of whom he had heard several times in his wanderings. He was said to be a master worker in wood and stone and metal whose achievements dazzled all who saw them. The work of his hands adorned churches and castles, and his name was known from Rome to Santiago, and north to Cologne. For the columns of a cathedral, he had chiseled heroic stone figures twice human size, of a beauty and fidelity that took the viewer's breath away; as a gift to an archbishop he had carved a crowded crucifixion scene on a piece of boxwood no bigger than a walnut. He had wrought reliquaries and sacred vessels of astonishing intricacy and delicacy, and monuments that crushed the ground beneath them. His imagination seemed to have no limit, and he had the skill to bring his imaginings to vivid life.

In a plain house on a quiet back street in a city of middling size Beran at last found Master Bruno's workshop. He entered the courtyard through a small door that stood open in the main gate, and proceeded unchallenged to a building at the far end from which came the sounds of hammer and chisel. The air inside was thick with dust and heavy with the pungency of paint and glue over the clean odor of wood. Two young men, apprentices to judge by their age, labored at a slab of stone; another mixed paints; a boy sharpened a chisel with painstaking care, with a dozen more beside him awaiting his attention. In a corner, seated at a workbench with a silver chalice in his hands, was a stocky man whose brown hair and beard were streaked with white. Beran went to him.

"Master Bruno?" he asked.

"I am he. And you?"

"My name is Beran. I've heard of your work, and I want you to make something for me."

The artisan climbed down from his stool and looked over his visitor. Beran's garments were of fine stuff, and he was well spoken and direct in his manner. The dust of the late-summer roads lay on his boots and in the folds of his cloak. He had traveled some distance, then, and come directly to the workshop. He was no commoner. He might have been a guildsman, or the servant of a powerful lord, or a Church official.

"If you want anything from me, you'll have a long wait for it," Bruno said at last.

"I'm willing to wait."

Bruno's manner softened a little. He had grown accustomed to self-importance on the part of his visitors. Beran's easy manner surprised him and impressed him favorably. "Well, then, what is it you want?"

Beran flicked aside the cloak and held out his right arm. "I want a hand. I heard of a reliquary you once made, a silver hand and forearm to contain a saint's bones. Can you do the same for the living?"

Without a word, Bruno beckoned him closer. Beran drew back his sleeve and laid his forearm on the workbench. Bruno carefully unfolded the cloth that covered it and inspected the stump. "When did you lose it?"

"About ten months ago."

"It's healed well. Does it give you any pain?"

"Not anymore, unless I strike it against something."

"But you feel the fingers moving sometimes, don't you?" said Bruno, looking at him expectantly.

"Yes. How do you know that?"

"I had an assistant some years ago, lost his hand when a rope broke on a slab of granite. Crushed his arm to a pulp, right to the elbow. He told me he could still feel his hand and fingers even when they were gone, and they hurt so much he thought he'd lose his mind."

"What became of him? Did the pain ever stop?"

"He took to drinking. They found him in the river one morning. Fell in, people said. The priest gave him Christian burial." Bruno looked at his visitor as if anticipating his response.

"Fingers that I don't have can't hurt me much," Beran said, "and I'm careful to stay away from the river when I drink."

"You're a sensible man. I wouldn't use silver, though. What you want is wood. I could make you a wooden hand with every joint you'd have in a real hand. It wouldn't work on its own, of course—nobody can make you a hand like that—but it could be useful for gripping things. Did you work with your hands before?"

"I was a juggler."

Bruno's thick brows went up and he winced. He shook his head slowly and let out his breath in a long, barely audible whistle.

"I don't miss it," Beran said. He told Bruno of his experience with Count Osostro. "He seemed determined to have my forgiveness, and he was generous with his gold. I can afford to pay you well."

Bruno waved his words aside. "I'd take everything that swine of a count had and then demand more, but from you I'll take only the price of my materials and two gold marks for my labor."

"You're generous."

The artisan laughed. "I'm not generous. I'm interested."

Beran took a room in a part of the city not far from the workshop. His window overlooked the river, and every morning when the weather was good, he walked along the embankment past the busy quays and on into the countryside, where the river ran smoothly and swiftly between high banks. It was not long before he was known to the boatmen and porters he met along the way, and when he told them of his reason for coming to the city, almost every one of them pointed out the place where the body of Bruno's assistant had been found. No two agreed precisely on the location, or on the true facts of the unfortunate young man's demise, but Beran listened to every account with a show of interest and belief. He repaid their stories with stories of his own, and became a welcome visitor wherever he went.

At the end of the second week after Beran's arrival, Bruno finished setting the stones in the silver chalice and then laid all other work aside to begin crafting the hand. He made Beran a partner in every step, from the selection of the wood through the carving and fitting of each joint to the final polishing. He explained the process, displayed his tools, and made Beran take up each one and try it on a piece of wood. Beran had long ago developed ambidexterity, and under Bruno's guidance he was able to carve a medallion with a design of grape leaves. It was a crude piece of work and he was the first to point out its flaws, but he was secretly quite proud of it.

Bruno had a Bible in his workshop, a fine volume for which he was to make a jeweled cover and a stand. When he saw Beran looking at the pages and found that Beran could indeed read the words, Bruno asked him to read to him and his men. Beren protested that he knew very little of letters, and had not attempted to read for some years, but Bruno and the workmen were persistent, and he gave in to them. At first he read haltingly, embarrassed to pause and stumble over words. But he improved each day, and to his pleasure he found his understanding increasing.

When he was not at Bruno's workshop, Beran spent most of his time at the inn, or nearby, with his acquaintances from the neighborhood. He often sat alone by the fire, or at his window, thinking and remembering. He had come to feel at home here, and he had the same appreciation of the quiet pleasures of the hearthside that he had felt the winter before. The thought of a wanderer's life, once so beguiling, no longer held attraction for him, but he had found nothing that attracted him more. This place was good and the people were friends, but he wanted something more, and he did not know what it might be.

As the work proceeded, Beran became a part of the little family in Bruno's workshop. The young apprentices appreciated his reading, enjoyed his stories, and admired what they saw as his courage. Though they never spoke of it except to joke, they were acutely aware of the hazards of their work, and all too familiar with the tale of the unfortunate assistant. Beran offered them an alternative to despair. He showed them that a man might suffer a devastating blow and yet go on, not surrendering, and not merely surviving, but constructing and enjoying a new life.

To the apprentices, Beran became an older brother, a model to set beside their master. To the master, he became a friend, and this he had not expected.

As they worked day after day in close proximity, Beran became aware of a growing respect on the part of the artisan, and it disquieted him, for he found it humbling. This was a new sensation for him. He had known admiration and praise, but never from one who aroused similar feelings in him. Now a man whose work would outlast his own life and the lives of all who knew him, and be seen and wondered at for as long as men and women could perceive beauty and feel awe and exultation and gratitude in its presence, was treating him as an equal. Bruno, who had devoted his life to creations that would endure, had sensed something worthy in a man whose energies had all been channeled into the ephemeral, whose greatest achievement was a gesture seen for an instant, enjoyed, and then stored carelessly in memory, to be recalled and reshaped to suit the mood of a moment; or, perhaps, to be forgotten as soon as seen.

Beran cherished the comradeship, but he could not understand it. He could only conclude that Bruno saw in him a remnant of what had once been present but now was gone and impossible to recapture: the hunger and dedication and love that drives a man to achieve. Beran's achievement might have been trivial, even ridiculous, but the impulse was an unmistakable mark, like a language or a creed, that joined all who bore it. Though he had tainted the gift, something of it still lived in him, and Bruno had caught a glimpse of it.

Beran left in the spring, and though he achieved all he had come for, the parting was painful for him. Beneath a soft black glove, he had a right hand that could be moved with all the grace and suppleness of flesh and bone. Bruno had fitted it with great care, and it was as comfortable as it was useful. With his left hand to press the lifeless fingers into the necessary configurations, Beran could hold a tool, lift a goblet, or carry light objects. With practice, his skill would grow.

. He left a good friend, and that saddened him. He had known partners, companions, admirers, and masters, but Bruno had been a friend and an equal. The feeling part of Beran longed to remain here with Bruno and the good men of the shop and all the companions he had come to know during his stay, but the thinking part of him knew that it was time to go. He had come to the city for a purpose, and that purpose was achieved. Perhaps he would return someday, but to stay would be to spoil the good that he had known here.

He left in the full glory of the spring, when all the world was coming to life. He had no goal and no destination, only an emptiness and a hunger for something he could not name. He felt like a blind archer standing on the brink of an abyss, drawing his bow to send an arrow into the void.

9

The
Innkeeper

The summer that followed was the finest in living memory. Wherever Beran rode, the sun was warm but never oppressive. The rains were gentle. They seemed to come only in the night and never linger overlong. Sun and rain together helped produce crops in such abundance that even the oldest could recall no harvest to match them.

The fall, too, was a time of great beauty, but as the days drew in and the nights grew longer, and the sun rose over frosted fields, and his breath hung white in the air before him when he set out of a morning, Beran once again sought a place to spend the winter. His feelings were mixed. After the summer's idle days and festive nights of outdoor delight, he looked forward to the quiet pleasures of the fading year: the warmth and companionship of the hearth, hot food and drink, song and story, the snug sensation of peering through a clear-rubbed spot on a window etched with frost to see the snow swirling outside and all the while to hear the logs crackling, hissing, settling into the embers. These were good things and he would enjoy them. But they would end when winter ended and he moved on to begin the yearly round again. Beyond the passing delights and comforts lay an emptiness that song and food and drink could not fill.

He rode by the river, past busy vineyards, and on through the forest, toward the mountains. On a blustery gray day with the promise of snow in the air, he came to a village at the foot of the mountains, where the road branched. He could go on into the mountains, or take the downhill road to the river. Or he might stay here.

An inn stood at the fork in the road. It was small, and no one was in sight, but something about it attracted him. He led his horse to the stable, entered the inn, and looked it over. It was empty, and silent, and he inspected it at leisure, liking everything he saw. The place was modest but spotlessly clean, with care given to every detail. He smelled a stew cooking and seated himself with pleased anticipation.

A dark-haired child peered through the sunlit doorway. He smiled at her and waved, but she was gone at once. A woman soon appeared. She paused in the entrance, as if surprised at the sight of him. Her figure was slender but sturdy. As she came near, he saw that she was young and attractive, with glistening chestnut hair that lay in clusters on her shoulders. The pallor of her face and the dark circles under her eyes made her seem older, but her greeting and her expression were animated and youthful.

"Good day to you, stranger," she said.

"Good day to you, mistress. I would like a bowl of the stew that smells so good, and some bread and cheese, and fruit, and ale."

"You shall have it at once," she said, and hurried from the room. She returned quickly with a large mug of ale and a half loaf of dark bread. Before Beran had taken more than a single sip and torn off a bit of bread, she was back with a bowl of steaming rabbit stew and a thick wedge of golden cheese. She stood anxiously by as he tasted the stew, and glowed with pleasure when he praised it.

After he had eaten, Beran told the woman that he planned to stay in the area for the winter, and asked if he might find accommodation here. She looked at him as if he had offered her a kingdom, and assured him that he might have his choice of three fine rooms here at the inn, each with its own fireplace and a comfortable bed, clean and quiet, just the sort of place to make a gentleman like him feel at home. The price she named was absurdly low.

Beran found the rooms to his liking. He doubted that

he would come upon better before winter closed in. He chose the largest of the three.

"Where is the master of the house?" he asked.

She hesitated for an instant before replying, "I am the master here."

"Indeed? You must be a busy woman. I saw no servants, yet the inn is clean and well run. Do you look after the child, too?"

"Marie-Jeanne is my daughter. My husband died last winter. I've kept the inn going by myself. It's hard work, but I manage." She shrugged, and said with a weary smile, "It must be done."

The room was cozy, the bed comfortable, and the meals excellent. The inn was full of the good smells of food and herbs. Beran settled in at once, looking forward to a pleasant winter. He expected the inn to be a gathering place and was surprised to find that it was not. Despite the isolation of the village, the excellence of the food and ale, and the woman's eagerness to please her guests, the inn was almost unfrequented. The occasional visitor stayed only briefly. Beran was curious, but it took him several weeks, much patience, and all his powers of cajolery to piece together the truth.

The woman's name was Anna. She was an orphan from a village on the other side of the mountain who had married the innkeeper four years before. The inn had been in the husband's family for three generations. It was a popular place when her husband was alive, but when he died on the mountain and Anna took on the running of it alone, even after she had been offered a generous price for it, the people of the village had turned their backs on her. Some resented her as an intruder. One man even hinted that the husband's death had been suspicious, though six people had seen him swept away in an avalanche. Others said that a woman could not and should not run an inn, and that it was wrong for a widow to have strangers living under the same roof with her and her child. From all that he heard, Beran gathered that someone was waiting for her to fail, in order to buy the inn at a good price.

Beran was no innocent. He had seen injustice, and dealt with people long enough to know that they could be small-minded, greedy, and cruel, but this display angered him. The more he learned, the angrier he became. This was none of his affair, true; but he could not force it from his mind.

Another, gentler emotion was mixed with his anger, and in time he was forced to admit to himself, reluctantly and with astonishment at his own feelings, that it was this unanticipated emotion that ruled him. He had admired Anna from their very first meeting. He had come to enjoy her presence more and more, and to take pleasure in playing with Marie-Jeanne, the little girl. His simple tricks with coins and nutshells delighted her, and the sight of her innocent happiness charmed him as no cheering crowd ever had.

The child liked him, he had no doubt. He was less certain about the mother's feelings. She treated him courteously, but he did not want to misinterpret her behavior. She might simply be showing politeness to a guest, or responding to his fondness for the child. They were often alone at the inn, and he had taken to helping her, for she worked incessantly and seemed sometimes to be on the brink of exhaustion. She always protested, and always gave in and allowed him to help just a bit. She never asked about his hand, and he did not speak of it.

In truth, he did not know how to tell her of his past. He had told his story scores of times, and now, for the first time, he cared about how it might be received. He did not want Anna to pity him, and he feared she might do so. Even worse, she might look upon him with the scorn that some of his deeds deserved. And yet he could not lie to her.

Beran confronted the truth: He was in love with this woman. The fact—and he knew it was a fact—left him confused and uncertain, even a bit afraid. The word itself troubled him. He had used it freely in his tales and ballads of courtly life. He had known many women, high- and lowborn, and declared his love for nearly all of them, but neither they nor he had ever taken the word seriously. They had given each other an evening's pleasure and then gone their ways, and the words were only a part of the pleasure. He could not remember their names or their faces, and though the thought bruised his vanity, he was sure they did not remember his.

He felt differently about Anna. He wanted to help her, and keep her from suffering at the hands of her odious neighbors. He wanted to be near her, to hear her speak and watch her go about her daily rounds. He wanted to hold her and caress her, to make love to her, but not in a passing encounter to be enjoyed and forgotten, like a meal or a joke or a bottle of good wine. This was something much more than the grasping passion of youth, quickly roused and as quickly sated. He wanted to be with her always. She was what he had sought without knowing. He felt the void in his life fill when she was near, and gape when they were apart. He wanted her, needed her, cared desperately for her happiness and well-being.

But he could not be sure of her feelings toward him. He suffered like a lovesick boy. Anna was so strong, so self-reliant, that she might see the attentions of a cripple—and Beran was painfully aware, for the first time, that he was a cripple, less able than she—as an insult, and reject him, even laugh at him. She might have no feelings for him at all, and no need or desire for his affection. He ached to declare himself, whatever the cost, but fear and doubt kept him silent. He, who had held great men and ladies spellbound with his words, silenced raucous mobs with his wit, did not know how to tell this woman of his true feelings. He pondered, and rehearsed speeches, and was silent.

One winter morning he awoke early. Unable to get back to sleep, he dressed, threw a blanket over his shoulders, and went downstairs in the dark. There he saw Anna asleep at a table before the dying fire. Papers were strewn about the table. He took the blanket from his shoulders to cover her, and she started awake at his touch. He saw the traces of tears on her face and knelt beside her.

"Tell me what's wrong, Anna. Let me help you."

"No. No, I mustn't."

"Anna, I want to help you."

"I mustn't bring trouble on you, not you, of all people."

All restraint vanished at the sight of her tears, and the note of pain in her voice. "Trouble? How could it trouble me to help you? I care for you deeply, and I want to do everything I can for you," Beran said before he was aware of his words. She looked at him, astonished, and he laughed and nodded and touched her face with his fingertips. "Yes, I love you, Anna! I'm able to say it at last!"

She fell into his arms sobbing, and he found his own eyes filling, even though he could not recall ever being happier. They stayed in each other's embrace for a long time, silent, and at last Beran said, "Tell me everything, Anna. Whatever is wrong, we'll find a way to make it right."

At those words she shook her head helplessly and began to cry, and he comforted her until she was able to speak. Her words poured out. She gestured to the papers on the table and said, "I wanted to keep the inn. Not for my sake—I did it for Frederick's memory and for the child. It seemed wrong to turn it over to others. The work was hard, and it got harder and harder, but I felt that I must do it. They offered me a lot of money—two hundred crowns, Beran, two hundred crowns in gold!—but I refused. I'm strong, and willing to work, and people liked to come here. It's a good inn. But they stayed away, all but a few. When you came, I thought things were changing, but it was just the same. I had to borrow, and now they want their money, and I have nothing. I don't understand how it happened, but I've lost everything I tried to save. I'll have nothing. And I'm so weary, Beran, I've worked so hard and I can't go on any longer."

He smiled and stroked her cheek, wiping away the tears. "You should have asked twice as much for my room."

"I couldn't have done that!"

"It would have been a fair price."

"But I wanted you to stay."

"I would have stayed, Anna. Once I saw you, I would have stayed at any price."

"I was afraid you'd leave when you saw no one coming here. You'd think something was wrong. I didn't want you to go."

"You need never worry about that again. I'm here, and I'm staying. Now, let's see what we can do about your trouble. May I look at these papers?"

"Oh, please! Can you read and do figures? Frederick was teaching me, but I was never good at such things. And he never really had time. There was always so much to do, and the child."

Beran pictured her husband, this man he would never know, and he was harsh in his judgment. He imagined a man perhaps a little kinder than the rest, sincere in his affection, wanting to trust, but nevertheless cut from the same cloth as his neighbors. He saw a man torn between the need to make his wife a partner and the fear that, given the chance, she might outshine him; a man who offered and then drew back, promised and then reneged, saw what ought to be but lacked the resolve to do what others had not done before him. Entangled in his own uncertainties, victim of his own fears, he had done worse than nothing. He had taught Anna just enough to confuse her and make her vulnerable to those who would cheat her of everything.

The papers confirmed Beran's suspicion. They were carefully and cleverly written, and it took a practiced deceiver to unravel their true intent. Anna had been lent small sums of money at usurious rates, but in such a way that no one could be accused of usury. She had trusted and been betrayed. Now she was being pressed for an outrageous amount, and offered the option of selling the inn and its contents in settlement of the debt, plus twenty crowns in gold.

"Do you know how much this inn is worth?" Beran asked.

"Frederick never spoke of it. The miller offered me two hundred crowns."

"It's worth four hundred. Maybe more. And now he wants to give you twenty crowns and cancel a debt that's been inflated tenfold."

"But what am I to do? He has papers. . . . I don't understand how it happened, Beran, but he has papers and documents. He's spoken to the magistrate."

"There's always a solution, Anna. We must think about it for a time. But before another day passes, I want to tell you about myself. I want you to be my wife, and you know nothing about me. You should not marry a man whose past is a secret.

"Oh, Beran, I'd marry you no matter—You don't have wives already, do you?" she asked in sudden dismay.

"Not one, not ever. I never wanted to marry before, Anna, never in all those years. Now I want only to be your husband and Marie-Jeanne's father." The domestic terms sounded sweet to his ear. Once he had thought them simple and even a bit foolish. Now he savored them as titles of honor.

He told Anna everything about his life except for his pact with the old man. That, he had decided, need never be told to anyone. It was over and done with, canceled out by the loss of his hand, and now as if it had never been. His story lasted through dawn and into daylight, and with Marie-Jeanne on his lap, eating a crust of bread and looking up at him in fascination, he told of his meeting with Bruno and the making of his new hand.

"And then I came here and met you two fine ladies, and I've never been happier in my life," he concluded.

"I'm happy too. All those roads, all that wandering . . . and at last you found us."

That day Beran took a long, solitary walk in order to think out a way to help Anna and prepare for their future together. They would leave this mean and narrow village and go somewhere better. An inn of their own seemed to him a fine idea. He knew a place in Bruno's city that would suit them perfectly, and if that place did not please Anna, he was sure there were many others. He could do some of the work, and a hired man could do whatever required two hands. He would teach Anna to keep accounts like a steward, and they would attend to all business matters together. Beran recalled how little he had regarded Albert's offer to teach him, and how valuable it was turning out to be, so much more valuable than what he had given in exchange. He shook his head in wonder at the way the things we prize turn out to be so trivial, and the things we dismiss become the mainstays of our lives. He had learned much that was useless, and some things that were wicked. Only now was he finding out what really mattered. He consoled himself with the thought that once he and Anna were settled, some of his experience, at least, would be an asset. He would see to it that every visitor had a fine time and left full of good things to say about their inn and its proprietors.

He returned to Anna with a plan. When he explained it, he could scarcely restrain his laughter. She was frightened at first; then she was reluctant. But as he talked on, her trust in him overcame her fears. Still with slight misgivings, but with confidence in Beran and a wonderstruck delight in his audacity, she agreed to his plan.

Next day, in freshly brushed garments and polished boots, an imposing silver medallion around his neck, Beran paid a visit to the miller's house. There had been much speculation in the village about his identity and the true purpose of his presence among them. Everyone had heard his story. They did not disbelieve him, but they all suspected that there was some deeper reason for his coming, which would be revealed at the proper time. The miller was more curious than most, since Beran was staying at the very inn on which he had long had designs. He received Beran with cautious courtesy.

Beran laid before him the papers taken from Anna, and after a sociable glass of wine and a polite and lengthy discussion that led nowhere, he laid beside them, without a word, the letter he had been given by Count Osostro. Written in elegant script on fine vellum, signed with the count's own hand and bearing his massive seal, it was an impressive document. It had been intended as a safe-conduct, but in his deep remorse the count had made the protection it conferred so sweeping that one might reasonably read into it a charter conferring the power of his own name on the bearer.

The miller, a squat, paunchy man in his middle years, perused the letter and then looked up at Beran, examining him more carefully than he had at first. "I have never heard of this man," he said.

"That surprises me. I should think that anyone who has dealings in the neighboring towns would know the name of Count Osostro. His residence is many days from here, but his power extends far."

"What has he to do with me?"

"The count is concerned with the treatment of widows," Beran said. He felt this to be a true and honest statement, considering the number of widows the count had created. "I have been investigating the situation at the inn. Your name and your signature appear on these documents."

"I have broken no law! This count of yours has no authority over me. Brise of Allfen is my lord."

"The name is familiar. I have heard it often at the court of Count Osostro, and always spoken with respect." Beran smiled. "The count values the cooperation of his friends and vassals in the pursuit of justice."

"Why do you accuse me? What have I done? I lent the woman money in her need, and now I want repayment."

"For a loan of thirty crowns you would take a property worth four hundred."

"I offered her money, too. I am under no obligation to do that. Considering the situation, I've been generous. The widow will have twenty crowns, and I'll find work for her at the inn. She never mentioned that, did she?"

Beran shook his head slowly, as one might at a child's fantastic explanation of some blunder. He frowned. "The count might feel that your demands are excessive. He is severe with usurers."

The word had a perceptible effect on the miller. He raised his hands before him and waved them as if to sweep it from the air. "I would never stoop to usury! I abominate usurers. I only tried to help a widow."

"I will tell him so," Beran said.

"What would the count do? Surely he would hear all the facts, and judge fairly."

Beran slowly peeled the glove from his right hand and held out the rigid fingers. "I once acted without the count's permission. He saw fit to strike off my hand. My actions turned out to be sound, so he also rewarded me for my good service. He is eminently fair." As he spoke, he folded back the wooden fingers one by one, making a fist. "And eminently just."

His eyes fixed on the hand, the miller said, "I meant to discuss the matter further with the widow. If there has been a miscalculation, an honest error in computing the debt—"

"You've already spoken to the widow, and your words were deceitful. Speak to me, and speak now," Beran said in a voice cold as iron.

The inn, with most of its contents, was sold to the miller for three hundred and sixty crowns and the cancellation of all debts. The miller also agreed to provide a wagon and two horses to convey the widow's goods, and assist her in every way.

Beran returned to the inn well pleased. The count's letter and his own talent for dissembling had been put to good use. Anna and the child were safe, and their future was clear. He could not help but ponder the curious working out of events. The count Osostro's careless cruelty had quit him of a promise that threatened to damn him. And when, for some unfathomable reason, the count had repented the deed, he had been wrung with remorse and showered gifts on the man he had already done a great good. Beran dwelt for a time on the bewildering paradox of the count's behavior, and then, being neither ironist nor philosopher, he concluded that great men behave in ways that common folk cannot understand, and dismissed the matter from his mind. It was wisest not to question one's blessings.

Anna, Beran, and Marie-Jeanne left the village in the fall and arrived in Bruno's city while the weather was still mild. Anna and Beran married as soon as could be arranged, and settled in a small house by the river.

The following summer, after much negotiating, they purchased an inn. It was a place well known to Beran from his earlier stay. The owner's health was failing, and he had decided to sell. The location was good, the building sturdy and roomy, but it had been carelessly maintained for the past few years and there was much work to be done.

Together, Anna and Beran made the inn flourish. Anna knew all there was to know about running a kitchen, ordering supplies, and managing servants, and Beran kept their guests cheerful and made them eager to return. Bruno and his assistants presented them with a magnificent carved door, and came often to the inn, where they were always welcome. Away from the scene of unhappy memories, Anna flourished, and seemed to grow younger. Their inn was a merry and a pleasant place. In their second year of marriage, they had a daughter, whom they named Annette. She was a beautiful child, Marie-Jeanne's pet, and the darling of all who came to the inn.

Beran settled comfortably into the roles of husband, father, and innkeeper. He was no longer gaunt, and his clothing was of good cut and material, though never gaudy. He had the appearance of a man very much at ease in his world. Busy and content, he found the time passing quickly. One day was much like another, and very little seemed to change but the two girls, who were more beautiful to his eyes each time he saw them. He thought of Marie-Jeanne as his own daughter, and she had long accepted him as her father. She would soon be at an age to marry, and Annette was less than five years younger. Between them and Anna and his work at the inn, he was too happy with the present to give thought to the past. It was over and behind him. He seldom thought about those days, and hoped that in time he would forget them completely.

On a night in early spring, when the roads were still barely passable, a man stopped at the inn. Beran welcomed him, eager to hear his news. The stranger's travels had taken him through the lands once ruled by Count Osostro, and in the course of conversation he mentioned the count's death. Beran, who had heard nothing of it, was curious, and asked to hear the story.

"They say it was a fever, but I know otherwise," said the traveler. He looked around the inn, and then, though there was no one to overhear, he drew his bench nearer to the table, leaning forward, drawing Beran closer as if in conspiracy. "I have an old friend whose daughter is wife to the brother of one of the guards who found the count that last night. Horrible, it was. He was clawed to bits."

"Clawed?"

The traveler nodded. "His flesh all torn. Strips of it hanging loose like rags, and all done by his own hand. The guard had seen some bloody sights—he fought up north when the mountain tribes rose, and everyone knows the things that were done in those times—but this made him sick as a baby. Screamed about the hand, the count did, about his own hand. 'Take away the hand!' and 'Save me from the hand!' Terrible things."

"Were those his words?"

"His very words. The guard was outside the door. He heard them plainly."

Beran rubbed his right wrist. "The count once did me a service," he said.

The traveler leaned back and looked at him with sudden interest and suspicion. "You're one of very few, then, my friend. From all I heard, he was a cruel, hard man."

"Of that I have no doubt. But he freed me of a great burden."

Their conversation turned to other subjects, and after a short time, Beran left the stranger and went to his own quarters upstairs. For the next few days, his manner was distant and preoccupied. Anna was concerned, but she did not press him for an explanation.

On the fourth day after learning of the count Osostro's death, Beran took to his bed. He was crushed under a burden of shame and remorse, and fearful of what was to come. Others might be deceived, but he knew the truth behind the traveler's story. The count Osostro had not been guilty of his own death. It was Beran's severed hand that had taken vengeance. Had Beran spoken, the count might now be alive; but he had kept silent, allowing another to make the decision and suffer the penalty. He had murdered the count with his silence.

He had eaten very little since the news arrived; now he ceased to eat almost entirely. His sleep was rent with awful dreams. Awake, he was obsessed by thoughts of the severed hand, its flesh discolored, its nails blackened, making its way crablike through forest and meadowland, over mountains and across rivers, seeking him. It had torn the flesh of Osostro, punishing him horribly for his sentence. It might do the same to Beran. It might do something far worse. Perhaps it would rejoin itself, rotted and corrupted, to Beran's forearm and make him something no longer fully human, a monster that would turn on those who loved him. Beran felt his fate closing in on him: a hideous life, an ignominious death, and an eternity of punishment.

Anna grew more worried with each day, but he would say nothing to her. Finally, one morning, she took him in her arms, weeping, and begged him to tell her what had befallen him.

He looked up at her, and his sleepless red-rimmed eyes were filled with tears. "I can tell no one."

"But you will die!"

"I think I deserve to die," he said, and turned away.

"Don't say such a thing! If you've done wrong, I don't care. Think of me, and the children."

"I do. I want to spare you."

She sat at his side and took his good hand in hers. "Tell me, and let me help you," she said. "You're a good man, Beran. You gave me your help when I needed it. Now it's my time to help you."

"Someday. Not now," he said, shaking his head. "There is no help now." He closed his eyes and lay back.

She left him. When she went downstairs, she found an old man sitting at a table near the door. He was hunched with the weight of his years. He wore clumsy, thick-soled boots and a long cloak caked with dust. His staff leaned against the wall, and a pack lay on the floor by his feet. At sight of her he rose, took up his things, and said in a mild voice, "I would speak with your husband."

"My husband is very sick. I think he may die."

"I know of his sickness. Take me to him," the old man said.

She brought him upstairs at once. At the door of the bedroom, he turned to her and said, "We must be alone. Let no one disturb us."

She nodded and withdrew. The old man entered the room, closing the door behind him. He roused the sleeper with a touch of his staff.

Beran started at the sight of him. "You!" he cried. "How did you find me?"

"I never lost you."

Propping himself up, Beran said more confidently, "Why do you come to me now? I owe you nothing."

"You owe me a great deal," said the old man. "Have you forgotten our agreement?"

"That's all over. The agreement was broken."

Shaking his head like a disappointed parent, the old man said, "You know better than that. You have lost no power. All you have lost is your faith in my promise. You owe me the price you agreed to pay."

"You took the soul of Count Osostro. Isn't that enough?"

The old man gave a soft, silken laugh and waved his hand in a gesture of dismissal. "It is not so easy as that. You have no knowledge of what souls I capture and which ones escape me. That is not your concern. You pledged me yours."

Beran held up his wooden hand. "I owe you nothing. I offered my right hand as a pledge, and the hand is gone. I can juggle no more, and I rejoice at the loss."

"You have a fine hand to replace it."

"A wooden hand. And I'm glad to have lost my own. I'd gladly have sacrificed more—" Beran began, but he stopped abruptly, horrified, as he looked down and saw his forearm gone, and only the stump of his elbow. An instant later, his arm was missing to the shoulder.

"How much more would you have sacrificed? Your other arm?" the old man said, and Beran's left arm was gone. "Or perhaps your sight," and Beran cried out at the sudden dark that enfolded him. Helpless in the blackness, he heard the old man's soft laughter on all sides. "It is so much easier to talk of sacrifices than to make them. You are very fortunate. You have sacrificed nothing."

Beran saw again, and his arms and hands were as before. The old man stepped closer to the bed. He extended his empty hand, fingers spread wide. He made a fist and opened it again. Caught between his fingers were four glistening black balls.

"You can juggle these."

Beran gave a wild laugh at the absurdity of his words. "Do you think me a fool? I've lost my hand! A man can't juggle with a wooden hand, however cleverly it's made, however much he may—"

The old man let the four black balls fall into his palm and then tossed them to Beran, who caught them instinctively and, with a fluid continuation of the catching motion, began to juggle them with all his old skill. There were five, then six balls, and then a seventh, an eighth, and more and more, all arcing smoothly between his two good hands. They changed shape and color, and Beran found himself juggling cubes and rings, daggers and spinning balls of colored flame, sacks of coins, crowns and scepters, rubies and diamonds and skulls, and other things not easily described. And then, at last, only four shining black balls.

"You see? I kept my bargain. You will keep yours," said the old man.

Beran flung down the balls, and they vanished before they touched the floor. "We have no bargain!" he cried. "This is more of your trickery."

"Trickery? You saw and felt each object. You felt your fingers move. You may wish to go on deceiving yourself, but our bargain remains."

"You are a mountebank."

"You know who I am," said the old man. "Perhaps you prefer not to admit it to yourself, but you know."

Beran avoided his eyes. "Whoever you are, we have no bargain."

"Oh, but we do. You have your old skill, which you thought lost. You saw and felt every object. You felt your fingers move. You may continue to deny it, but our bargain stands. Because of the inconvenience you have suffered, I will overlook your attempt to cheat me, and demand no more of you than before. In fact. . . ." The old man paused and shut his eyes thoughtfully for a moment, and then, raising a forefinger, said, "I will ask less. I am not a harsh master." With a sweeping gesture betokening largesse, he said, "Your soul is yours. I relinquish all claim to it, on one condition: Win me a soul I might not have gained otherwise. Do this, and your debt to me is paid. It is a fair offer."

"Fair indeed. I need only send a stranger to damnation."

"You need not seek far. There are always prospects at the inn. There are your daughters. . . ."

"You will never have them!"

"That is not for you to say. They are beautiful creatures, with long lives before them and many choices still to make," said the old man mildly. "But if the thought is uncomfortable, we will leave that up to time and the ladies themselves. Your wife is an amiable woman. Her soul would satisfy me."

"I will never betray those I love," Beran said, but he knew in his heart that fear might make him do anything, even this. He could not resist the old man, however hard he might try. He could feel evil rising like a dark tide all around him. In the end, the old man would have his way.

The old man laughed, a soft, dry whisper of mockery that seemed to multiply upon itself, echoing and re-echoing and forcing back the walls until the little chamber was an unbounded blackness throbbing with his crescent laughter. His face bloated and twisted, and his grin and leering eyes were terrible to see. He swelled to enormous size. His hands were great as galleys, and wailing naked figures rose and criss-crossed in an arc from hand to hand as he juggled an innumerable multitude of lost souls that slipped between the fingers one by one to pour like sifted grain into an unseen abyss. Beran groaned and covered his eyes, but he could not hide from the wailing and the laughter and the voice that thundered, "You will find an innocent soul, and you will render it fit for my possession. Do this, slave, or forfeit your own." Then there was silence, and when Beran dared to look, the old man was gone.

10

The
Pilgrim

is first thought was *They must not know.* He lay for a long time, unable to move, drained of his strength and feeling, drenched in sweat and shuddering from a sickness deeper than any fleshly ill. The past was not behind him—it was here, present, real, and inescapable. He had not redeemed himself, only deluded himself. With a single visit and a few words the old man had wrenched his life apart and reshaped it into something monstrous, worse than before. From a figure of love and protection he had been made into an agent of damnation.

And immediately he saw the inevitable consequence: *I must leave them. I must go far away, or I may destroy them forever.*

He loved his wife and children more than anything he had ever known before, but he knew how weak a man could be, and what kind of man he had once been and might be again. He could be strong for a time, but in the end, forced to choose between suffering and betrayal, he feared that he would weaken. It was a terrible thought, a recognition of something in him so foul as to be physically revolting. It might be true of all men, or a wretched few, or of him alone. That did not matter. It was true, and it imposed on him a duty that he could not evade.

He must leave Anna and their children. He was their enemy, and he had to get as far from them as he could. Painful as that would be for all of them, to stay would be far worse.

He tried to think of some way to leave without causing unnecessary pain. Simply to steal away was unthinkable; in their innocence, they would blame not him, but some trifling fault in themselves, and feel a guilt they did not deserve. To lie was to start down the path to his old life, the life that had brought him to this; yet to tell the truth would be to reveal himself as an unholy thing, a tool of evil, a damned soul beyond all hope of mercy. It was pain enough to know that he must see them no more; he did not want to lose their love.

Anna entered the room so quietly that he was unaware of her presence. When he did not speak, she asked, "Did the old man help you?"

He blinked and started up, propping himself on an

elbow. He wanted to cry out, to laugh at the awful irony of her words, to curse the old man and himself; but he was too weak and empty for such an outburst. He sighed and shook his head. "He didn't come to heal me, Anna, only to talk. I knew him once, a long time ago."

And then the solution came to him, and he knew that he must speak now, before he had time to think, and weaken, and lose his resolve. He reached out and took her hand. "Do you remember the traveler who came the other night, the one I spoke with for such a long time?"

"The bearded man in the patched cloak?"

"Yes. When I spoke to him, and again as I talked with the old man, I was reminded of my past life. I did terrible things when I was young, Anna. I've put them out of my memory all these years, but I can ignore them no longer. I must make atonement. I must go on pilgrimage."

She was stunned by the suddenness of this momentous decision, and could not speak for a time. She sat on the bed, holding his hand, and at last said, "I never knew you to be dishonest, or to do a cruel thing. You've been a good man."

"You've helped me to be better than I ever thought I could be. But the past remains. I must atone for what I did before, or my punishment will be great."

"You're too weak to travel. You must be in good

health to go on pilgrimage. You need all your
strength."

"I won't leave until I regain my health. I feel much
better simply having made my decision."

"Where will you go?"

He had not considered a destination, but he hesitated only briefly before saying, "The Holy Land."

She pressed his hand. This was the great pilgrimage,
the richest in grace and blessings, the longest and the
most perilous. The land route was no longer open to
travelers, and the sea voyage was notorious for the
hardship and dangers involved. Beran would be long
absent. He might never return. But it was not lawful to
restrain a man once he had decided on a pilgrimage to
the Holy Land. In all other cases, a man or woman
could not depart on pilgrimage without a spouse's consent, but one who had the call to the Holy Land was
not to be impeded. Anna knew that her own desires
and needs, and those of their children, paled beside
Beran's hope of salvation.

"You will be gone for a long time," she said. "I'll
need someone to help me here."

"Our daughters are dependable. And the servants
are good workers, and loyal. You've taught them well.
Marie-Jeanne will be ready to marry before long, and
her husband will be able to help."

"But you're the one who's made us successful."

He smiled and shook his head. "I do little but talk

and exchange tales with our visitors. They leave here marveling at the food and the ale and the softness of the beds, and the cleanness of the place, and the three beautiful women who run it all so well. The inn will prosper without me."

She threw her arms around him. "But you'll be gone for such a long time! And what if you don't return? Many men set out on pilgrimage and never come back."

"I must go, Anna. I'm not fit to remain here as I am."

Anna saw nothing but good in her husband, but she dared not dispute his words, for she knew that even the saintliest of men and women was born into sin and the never-ending struggle to resist it. Blessed was the man who was vouchsafed a glimpse of his soul and given the chance to purge himself of the punishment that awaited him after death. Even when one had repented and confessed, the stain of evil remained, and pilgrimage was the hope of a second baptism, a spiritual rebirth into innocence.

The suddenness of Beran's decision did not surprise her. The call to pilgrimage, she knew, might come at any time, unsought and unanticipated. She had heard many accounts, and she believed them. Warriors had ridden from the field in their hour of triumph; brides and bridegrooms had left the marriage chamber, merchants abandoned their counting tables, invalids risen from their sickbeds, the rich and powerful forsaken their wealth and titles to take up the way of the pilgrim. And woe to those who turned a deaf ear to the summons, or those who persuaded another to delay, or temporize, or ignore the call. Beran had to leave them; and with her inherent good sense, Anna told herself that the sooner he left the sooner he would return, and began to prepare for his departure.

His daughters were divided in their feelings. It was a good and holy thing to have one's father go on pilgrimage, and they were young enough to relish the excitement it would cause at the inn and among their neighbors. But Beran had been a good father, kindly and generous to them, always willing to listen and able to cheer them up even when they were most downcast. They did not want him to go away and place himself in danger, and perhaps never return to them. But they soon persuaded themselves that he would return, and return quickly, and have tales to tell of strange lands and their ways, and bring them fine gifts from the other side of the world.

On the afternoon of the old man's visit, Beran ate heartily for the first time in days. He was up early the next morning, eager to build the strength needed for departure. He wanted no more delay. The sooner he left his wife and daughters, the sooner they were out of danger.

During the days of preparation, he had time to think about the old man's sudden appearance. With the clarity of hindsight, he realized that there had been warnings. Only a week earlier there had been a sudden high wind that rattled the shutters of the inn and caused the door to slam loudly. Some of those present had crossed themselves, for they knew that such winds could be a sign of the adversary's presence, but Beran had dismissed the episode lightly, even when he saw the trees blown down near the churchyard. And in the spring he had heard of a pack of savage black dogs attacking a child in a nearby village. If only he had heeded such warnings, he might have prepared himself to confront the old man.

And as he pondered, he realized that even a clear warning would have been little help to him. What could he have done? He had never spoken of his pact to the priest, for fear that the good man would expel him from the Church if he knew of it. For years he had kept his secret, telling himself that with his hand gone, the past had been wiped out and his score settled. He had done no penance and closed his mind to the thought of atonement.

Now he saw the delusion he had practiced on himself. The power of evil is tenacious. One who has embraced it willingly and lived long in its grip does not escape in an instant. Like dye, the evil penetrates every fiber of his soul, and can be cleansed—if cleansed at all—only slowly and laboriously. His hand was restored, the wood given quickness and motion, a clear sign that his soul was unchanged, the old evil abiding in it, waiting only the summons of its master to show itself forth. His deliverance had been a deception. He had been in thrall to the old man all that time. If he was ever to be free, he must do something more.

The pilgrimage took on new significance in his mind. He had thought of it on the spur of the moment, but he came to see that he had actually been inspired. It was no longer merely an explanation for his leaving Anna and the children; it was his hope of redemption. The old man had made the wood come alive and given back the power in his hand, but Beran would reject that evil gift. The hand itself was a sign of his past sins; that was what gave the enemy power over it. He would bind the fingers tightly, and if a day came when he was purged and cleansed and fit to look upon his wife and children, he would cast off the hand forever.

On the fifteenth day after the old man's visit, Beran donned the weeds of the pilgrim, took up the scrip and bourdonnée, and resumed his wanderings, setting forth alone early on a fine spring morning. He had said his farewells, made peace with any he had offended, and turned over all his goods to his wife and daughters. He had not confessed. He told himself that he was not yet ready to be shriven, but he knew that he did not dare to speak his soul's state aloud. His right hand was tightly bound in a clean white wrapping that immobilized it. He took with him only the clothes on his back, a day's food, and money to pay for his passage. For all else, he was resolved to earn his way or beg.

The cost of a pilgrimage to the Holy Land was substantial. Beran had no lord to lend him the sum and no wealthy patron to share in the merits of the pilgrimage by assisting him. He would not consider selling the inn. Besides, to carry the amount required for all the tolls, fees, and bribes, his passage and provisions, was to subject oneself to constant anxiety and fear, and risk the loss of it, and of one's life as well. A pilgrim could depend on alms and the care of the pious. For the rest he put his trust in God.

There were those who believed that solitary pilgrimage was specially meritorious, but Beran knew the dangers of the road and intended to join with companions as soon as he could. It was not difficult to find others to travel with, but one had to be certain first of all that they were legitimate pilgrims, and this was not always easy to do. Thieves often dressed as pilgrims and even as friars, and presented a friendly and pious front to an unsuspecting traveler. And even if one found honest, godly folk, they might not be good companions. To travel with those who walked too slowly, or too fast, or who wished to sing and chatter and make merry when one wished to think or pray— or vice versa—was sure to create unpleasantness and generate uncharitable thoughts. He traveled for eight days and nights alone, and on the ninth day, at a monastery, he joined a band of twenty pilgrims on their way to the same destination.

They faced all the hazards he had known in his youth, and some he had avoided until this time. Thrice they were forced far out of their way by swollen rivers, once by a bridge that had washed away only hours before their arrival. When they forded the river, one of their number was swept away by the raging waters, and his body never found. They dragged their way through ankle-deep mud in the forest, and lost another companion in an attack by bandits. They were often hungry and thirsty, cold at night, wet sometimes for days on end. Even though as pilgrims they were exempt from tolls in all Christian lands, and most of them displayed the badges of earlier pilgrimages as proof of their right, they were threatened and man-handled and more than once turned back from a ford or bridge.

They had good experiences as well as bad. Priories and abbeys offered them shelter and hospitality. They were not of a rank to be welcomed in the palaces of the great, but lesser personages were willing to open their gates to them. Once, at a manor house, as he sat on the ground in the beggars' row awaiting such fare as might be distributed, Beran recalled his treatment in far more splendid halls, when he performed before the high table and was rewarded with praise and gold. He accepted the change in his fortunes willingly and took courage from it, for it showed him that he had left at least one aspect of his old life behind, and thus might hope to abandon the past entirely.

Holy men along the way guided and aided them, offered shelter and sometimes food. A hermit helped them to cross a river in flood, risking his own life repeatedly to aid them. People gave them food or alms according to their means. One evening in a dense wood a band of thieves came upon them but repented of their bad intent before a blow was struck. Instead they shared their food with the pilgrims and kept watch with them during the night. In the morning, when the others returned to their forest lair, two of the thieves remained. They knelt to pray with the pilgrims and asked to join the band. After much discussion, they were accepted. Beran carried the day for them when he pointed out that the two penitents restored them to their original number, and this should be taken as a sign of favor.

Beran spoke with the two newcomers along the way, and found that they were men more unfortunate than malevolent. The older, a man close to Beran's age, had been unjustly accused by envious neighbors who had sworn falsely against him; the other, an apprentice to a carpenter, had been badly beaten by his master, and had run away as soon as he was able. He still bore the markings of his ill-treatment on his face and shoulders. Neither man had wanted to rob or do harm to others, but the outlaw life had made them desperate and they had fallen in with others even more desperate than they.

"When I saw you by the fire, some of you praying, I couldn't strike a blow," said the apprentice. "It came clear to me, all of a sudden, that I must change my ways."

"I felt the same. The very same," said the other. "Almost as if I heard a voice telling me to lay down my weapon."

"We all felt it. I looked around at the others, and they were standing like statues, not able to move or strike. Some of them just slipped away without saying a word."

Jonathan, the leader of the company, said, "Perhaps you've shown them what they must do to save themselves. We must pray that they see their error, and turn to God."

They prayed fervently each day for that worthy intention. They were disappointed when the apprentice left them at the end of a week in their company, but consoled themselves with the obvious sincerity of the older man, whose name was Harik.

They now had to forage for themselves and take whatever shelter they could find, but once they had passed through the thickest forest, they hoped once again to spend the night under a roof. They were reluctant to mingle with the tipplers and merrymakers who might be found at a wayside inn. By mutual consent, they sought shelter only in monastery guest houses along the way.

For centuries, the monks had honored their obligation to provide pilgrims with shelter, fresh water, and bread. Their hospices were separate from the monastery proper, sometimes outside the precincts entirely. They were all alike in design, with a central hall opening into rooms in which several men slept, sometimes on a bed generously donated, more often on a pallet, or in straw heaped on the floor. In other respects the hospices differed greatly from one another. In a few the pilgrims were fed generously, in others they dined on crusts, and in some they had to find for themselves. In some of them the monks received those on pilgrimage as honored guests, and washed their feet; in others the pilgrims were scarcely noticed.

It was more common for the monks to be busy with, if not overworked by, their duties. The most valuable information Beran and his companions acquired was gleaned from conversations with other pilgrims, especially those returning from their journeys. All had much to tell, and all were willing to exchange it for news from home. At a hospice in the mountains, a palmer returning after eight years in the Holy Land spent two full days instructing them in languages that would make their way easier. He gave them words in Arabic, Turkish, Hebrew, and Greek, repeating them patiently, correcting their pronunciation until it was satisfactory. The pilgrims were grateful to him, for most of them spoke only their own tongue, and even Beran, for all his wandering, had learned no languages of the East. Beran was able to transcribe the words, which made their learning easier. They spent some time each day reciting the terms to one another and committing them to memory.

Another traveler gave them news that was equally valuable, but disquieting. He was a gaunt, white-haired old German knight, his face and hands browned by desert suns, his garments threadbare, his hat covered with the badges of many pilgrimages. In his long lifetime he had visited Canterbury and Santiago, Rocamadour and Rome, and all the sites in the Holy Land. He had been as far south as Mount Sinai, to Jericho and across the Jordan, and north to Nazareth. He had endured sickness and near starvation, seen friends die by the roadside from heat and thirst and at the hands of the raiders who appeared from nowhere to strike and then vanish. He shook his head sadly at the memory.

"And not all the bandits were Arabs. I say it with shame; I saw Englishmen and Frenchmen—and Germans, too—preying on their fellow Christians, whom they should have been guarding."

"But I have heard that the Templars patrol the roads and defend the pilgrim," said one of the company.

"Ah, the Templars are true knights. You may trust your life to them. But others have turned to brigandage. They ride at the Arabs' side and outdo them in cruelty. I tell you this—it was an Arab chief nursed me back to health when Christians had robbed and beaten me and left me to die."

The German had much to tell them that was helpful, especially regarding travel by sea. This had often been discussed among the company, but never resolved. He was quite clear on the point: they must entrust themselves to no captains but the Venetians, and to no Venetian ship but a galley.

"The others are cheaper, but they're not seaworthy. I've heard of a Sicilian that sank like a stone when she was barely out of the harbor, and everyone aboard drowned. The Genoese and Pisans are good sailors with good ships, but they've been known to stop at an Arab port and sell their passengers to slavers. Trust to the Venetian galleys. They'll bring you there safely, and the captain will see to all that's necessary."

"What is the price of passage?" Jonathan asked.

"You will need one hundred ducats for each man, and you should get as much more as you can."

"Impossible!" cried Jonathan, as others shook their heads and expressed similar sentiments. "Some of us have come all this way with empty purses, as a pilgrim should. How are we to get all that money?"

The German was unmoved. "Beg for it. The Venetian captains are honest men. They'll treat you fairly, but they must be paid. For that price they will pay all the tolls and bribes and fees—and there are plenty. You must each pay one gold piece to enter Jerusalem, and you may be forced to pay more. There will be similar fees along the way."

"But if we cannot pay, surely—"

"Surely you will never reach your goal."

No one responded. This was not what the pilgrims had hoped to hear. Beran's heart sank, for he had brought only half that amount, and some of it was already spent. Many of the others had heeded the exhortation to travel in poverty, and now they were told that their very poverty might prevent them from reaching their goal, or endanger their lives should they somehow cross the sea.

They were downcast for a time, but they were not to be discouraged. If they must beg for their passage money, they would beg, and beg they did from then on. By the time they reached Venice, they had amassed only a third of the necessary amount, but they were astonished that they had been able to acquire that much. Their success inspired them to pursue their efforts ever more vigorously.

In Venice the company began to break up. They arrived in the middle of August, the day before the feast of the Assumption. The pilgrim fleet sailed twice each year, in September and March, and the autumn departure was the great topic of discussion in the port. Two of the pilgrims met old acquaintances whose ship was to set out on the morrow, and they made arrangements to depart with their old friends. The rest searched among the crowds for familiar faces and pursued their begging as best they could; but Venice was crowded with pilgrims, many of them in the same straits.

One of a pair of older pilgrims who had set out together fell ill and died in the care of the monks. The other collapsed with a fever, and Harik, who had become friendly with them, chose to stay to nurse him and depart with the spring fleet. As the days passed and little was added to their purses, some of the others began to waver from their earlier resolve to sail only in one of the galleys, which were safer but so much more costly. A smaller sailing ship, they learned, would carry them for as little as twenty ducats. True, they would be entirely on their own once they stepped ashore, but what did that matter if they were in the Holy Land? And as for safety, they placed themselves in God's hands.

Jonathan reminded them that while such an attitude might be pious, it might also be presumptuous, but they were impatient and not to be swayed. Seven of them contracted with the captain of a single-masted sailing ship, and Beran went with them to the quay.

As the ship diminished into the distance, a man turned to Beran and said, "If you have friends on that hulk, pray for them." He spoke Beran's language well, with the accent of a Venetian.

"Is it a bad ship?"

The man spat into the water. He held out his hands before him, palms facing, about two feet apart. "Rats that big. And if the rats don't eat them alive, they'll starve to death or drown." He brought his hands closer together, now barely a foot apart. "That much room for each man. Not enough to turn around, and you daren't stand up or you'll have your head knocked off by a boom."

"I was told to travel only in a galley," Beran said.

"Sound advice. Which one will you be on?"

"I don't know yet. I may not be able to leave until the spring."

The man spat again and shook his head vigorously. "You don't want to spend a winter in Venice, my friend. It's cold and wet. The sooner you get to sea, the sooner you'll set foot in the holy places."

"If I had the money, I'd leave today," Beran said.

"It doesn't take all that much," said the stranger.

"I met a man who was on his way back from the Holy Land. He said I'd need at least a hundred ducats."

The stranger laughed loudly. "Do you mean to travel with a couple of servants, and fill the hold with fine wines and roast meats? A hundred ducats! Buy your own galley and be done with it!"

"Can I find a place on a galley for less?"

"I can name a dozen captains who'll take you to Joppa and back for thirty ducats. There's Mezzana, Corsini. . . . Corsini is one of the best, and he may have room for a few more. I hear Priuli is filled up already. How many in your party? Are you traveling alone?"

"I have seven companions," Beran said.

The stranger pondered for a moment, moving his fingers as if to calculate the space required for eight pilgrims, and then said, "Talk to Corsini. Go to him right away, and he may be able to take you all. Come, I'll take you myself. It's not far. You can see the ship from here."

By that evening, Beran and his companions had met with Captain Corsini. The next day they signed a contract to sail in his galley, the *San Giovanni Evangelista*. They paid thirty ducats each, which left them enough to buy bedding and provisions for the voyage. Corsini was to provide food and water, but they had been warned about the amount and quality of shipboard food by everyone they met. Even the helpful acquaintance who guided them to Corsini—and who turned out to be one of the hands on the *San Giovanni Evangelista*—advised them to purchase food to supplement their shipboard fare, and was quite specific in his recommendations of what to buy, where to buy it, and how much to pay. With his assistance, they set out well prepared.

Their last days in Venice were busy. After months of slow travel on foot, sometimes managing no more than three miles in a day through the mud of the forest roads or the snow of the mountain passes, they were about to embark on the last stage of the journey. The next ground on which they set their feet would be the land where Christ and His apostles had walked, where saints had suffered and Crusaders fought, the land where every stone could tell a pious tale.

Weather delayed their departure for one day. They set out on a crisp September morning, with the sky cloudless and a fresh breeze blowing.

11

The
Hermit

With the excitement and bustle of embarkation behind them and weeks on the open water ahead, Beran, his companions, and the rest of the pilgrims found themselves struggling to cope in an unfamiliar world. Few of them had been on a seagoing ship before. Most were strangers to the sea, knowing of it only what they had learned from other travelers and from the gossip of the inn and hospice, and they looked upon the voyage with feelings ranging from eager curiosity to paralyzing fear.

For the first five days, as they headed south to the open waters of the Mediterranean, the weather was fair and the sea was calm. A few of the pilgrims had brief bouts of seasickness, but they recovered and were able to join with the others in prayer and the singing of hymns. A friar who was among them delivered learned sermons, some lasting for an entire afternoon.

But the friar's eloquence grew repetitive after a few weeks, and then became tedious. When the weather changed, he could not preach at all for the tossing and rolling of the ship. Even if he had tried, no one would have heard his words over the wind and sea and the shouting of the crew as they dashed back and forth over the decks. The pilgrims were preoccupied with holding on for dear life while their stomachs rebelled.

The crew were lively and cheerful whatever the weather. Their high spirits and patent lack of sympathy made the seasick pilgrims' suffering the harder to bear. The novelty of shipboard life quickly wore off, and all the pilgrims, sick and well, grew weary of what was to them the monotonous emptiness of sea and sky. Some accepted their lot patiently and endured in silence; others were loud in their complaint.

They complained about the ship's food and water, the rats and fleas, the heat of day and the chill of night, and the omnipresent and inescapable stench rising from the rowers' benches, where more than a hundred men sat chained in their own filth. They lamented their abandonment by the other ships in the fleet, which by now were specks in the distance. They bemoaned the cramped conditions aboard the *San Giovanni Evangelista*. There was no room on board to exercise; one could not take two normal strides without climbing over another passenger. Even standing at the rail was hazardous, for one might be pitched overboard by a crewman dashing on some errand. The crew seemed always to be in a hurry, always shouting and thrusting the pilgrims aside.

The pilgrims had sworn not to gamble, for that led to oaths and quarrels; nor to sing, for that was an invitation to bawdiness. Two of them played chess on the first few days of the voyage, but the others insisted that this was only a form of gambling and demanded that they put away the board and pieces or have them thrown into the sea. Tempers were shorter each day, and the mood ever more sour. The pilgrims talked to one another less and less. All were plagued with boredom. Beran kept to himself, to avoid quarrels, and so did most of the others. He felt sometimes as if he were on a ship of dead souls, each man isolated from his fellows, staring ahead with unseeing eyes, silent, listless, motionless, beyond all caring.

As the days slowly passed, each seeming longer than the one before, Beran often thought of unbinding his hand and using his skill to divert the crew and passengers and raise their spirits. No one on board knew of his juggling ability. They had all noticed his bandaged hand, but no one asked about it, and he did not volunteer an explanation. A pilgrim might tell as much or as little as he liked of his past, or he might say nothing at all. Beran had chosen to say nothing.

With very little to distract him, his deliberations occupied most of his time and delved into every facet of the question. He knew that even the simplest display of his juggling would astound all on board and give them something to talk about and to anticipate each day. It would be a good thing to cheer up his companions and make them feel more kindly toward one another and the crew. He would provide pleasure for all with no risk of gambling or quarrels or other unsuitable behavior. The friar might find in his juggling an allegorical significance worthy of a sermon. To make others happy was a good deed. To create goodwill where there was impatience and anger was a charitable act. To offer innocent diversion was to occupy his companions' minds in a harmless way, and thus guard them from idle thoughts and temptations. Beran had sworn to himself that the hand would remain bound, but he had not taken a solemn vow before the altar. Such a promise as he had made could surely be revoked for so many worthy motives. So he reasoned.

Against these positive arguments stood the fact that his right hand was an accursed gift and his juggling skill came from the same tainted source. Was it possible for any good to come from them? Might he not be loosing the enemy among his fellow pilgrims, delivering them into his hands when their lives were at risk every instant from the sea and pirates, and when the

Holy Land and the purging of their sins were only weeks away?

For many days he prayed and agonized over his decision. It might be an impulse of good or a temptation to evil, and he could not decide which. In the end, he left his hand bound, persuaded at last that while he might give relief and pleasure to others by a display of his juggling, he would also give them to himself. That would be wrong, for he was a penitent. He deserved neither relief nor pleasure.

The pilgrims were free to go ashore when the ship stopped for provisions, but they soon found that one port was much like another and that pilgrims were looked upon as fair game in all of them. The diversion of setting foot on unfamiliar ground was offset by the importunings and occasional thievery of the inhabitants. After the first stop, many of the pilgrims remained on board. At Cyprus, all but a few flatly refused to go ashore, having been warned of the unhealthy air of Famagusta. The crew, who had long listened to their complaints about the stench arising from the rowers' benches, were much amused by this objection.

Two days out of Cyprus, five of the oarsmen fell ill from tainted food. Two died almost at once, in convulsions. The others writhed and groaned, crying out in agony, bodies contorted in pain, and died before sundown of the same day. The delay and loss of manpower caused the *San Giovanni Evangelista* to lag far behind the rest of the fleet. Three days from Beirut, having seen no other ship since the death of the last oarsman, they caught sight of a long, low galley in the distance. It appeared to be gaining on them. There was sudden excitement among the crew, and the word "Pirates" spread quickly.

The captain ordered the pilgrims to assemble. Three crewmen broke out weapons and began to distribute them to crew and passengers alike. Several of the pilgrims refused to take up arms, protesting that their pilgrim status exempted them from the obligation to defend the ship. The rest were eager for action.

"You may fight or not," said the captain, "but we have little chance of outrunning them with five oarsmen gone. If we're taken, we'll all end our lives in the galleys ourselves."

"But we will be ransomed!" a pilgrim cried.

The captain and several crewmen laughed. "Oh, have we princes among us? Or perhaps wealthy merchants whose friends are waiting in Venice with a hogshead of ducats? They'd better be quick about it," the captain said. He jerked his thumb toward the pirate ship and said, "Make those fellows wait too long for their money and they may send you back without your eyes, or your tongue."

That information was sufficient to persuade most of the protesters, who took up crossbows and cutlasses.

One husky man stepped forward and said, "I will not fight, but I'll pull an oar."

"If four more will join you, we may have a chance to get away," said the captain.

Four more pilgrims came forth. They were men Beran had not spoken to during the voyage; he did not even know their names. They stripped off their tunics and descended into the stench and filth of the rowing benches. Beran had a quick glimpse of faint stripes on the first man's back, and called out thanks and encouragement to him. Several of the others, passengers and crew, added their words to Beran's. The man acknowledged them with a wave of his hand.

Beran took a cutlass and stood by the rail, watching the pirate galley close the gap between them. It seemed to be gaining, but not as quickly as it had been. He felt a surge of hope.

The sailor beside him glanced down at Beran's bandaged hand and grinned. "You've seen some fighting, have you?"

Beran raised the cutlass. "I still have one good hand."

"You'd better use it well. You're no good at the oars. They'll toss you over if they take us."

That was something that had not occurred to Beran, and it reopened the question he had thought resolved. If they were taken, should he let himself be killed, or would it be right to unbind his hand and reveal his skill? Even the smallest display of his ability would make him too valuable to be killed outright. He might improve the lot of his companions, as well, and perhaps even win their freedom. Was it right for a man to make use of one evil in order to avoid another? Should he save his life at the risk of becoming a slave of some Turkish master? He felt a sudden flush of hot anger at his own weakness. He had not left everything he loved merely to survive at any price. He gripped the cutlass tightly, resolved to fight to the death and die, if need be, with his secret unrevealed.

In the event, they did not have to fight. With the five volunteers at the oars, the *San Giovanni Evangelista* held its distance from the pursuing galley, and when the lookout sighted a ship of the Venetian fleet ahead, they all cheered at their delivery. In a very short time the pirate broke off pursuit. The pilgrims and crew brandished their weapons and shouted defiance to cover their relief.

The remaining days at sea were uneventful, but none of the pilgrims now complained of monotony. They relived their narrow escape, gave thanks for deliverance, and looked forward eagerly to arrival.

In the busy, crowded port of Joppa, they waited impatiently while the captain attended to all the details, and the considerable expenses, of landing. Arab officials were waiting on the shore, on horseback, to receive the list of pilgrims' names and collect the toll for each one. The officials were ill-tempered and brusque, having dealt with two pilgrim ships before the arrival of the *San Giovanni Evangelista,* and the transaction was long, drawn out, and very noisy. Arab children swarmed about the waiting pilgrims, plucking at their robes and shouting incessantly in incomprehensible, shrill voices.

A delegation of pilgrims complained of the delay to the captain when he rejoined them. He listened patiently, frowning but offering no comment, and then in the most caustic terms informed them of their good fortune. Had the officials not been here, it would have been necessary to send to the Arab governor of Jerusalem and wait in Joppa for the arrival of his agents. Waiting pilgrims were kept in underground cellars in the town, which, while not actually dungeons, were vile and unhealthy places. They had claimed their toll of victims. After this information, there were no more complaints.

They set out at last on the Jerusalem road, escorted by mounted Arabs. The pilgrims, on donkeys, were instructed to keep close together. Stragglers were certain to be attacked by the bandits who lined the way, hidden in caves and crevices, behind rocks, awaiting the chance to swoop down, strike, and vanish before the alarm could be given. Seventeen unwary pilgrims had been slain in such a raid only a few days before. The road was said to be patrolled by Knights Templar, but the pilgrims saw none, though they looked eagerly for a sign of them.

Beran made his way to the side of the man who had first offered to take a place among the oarsmen. "I must thank you. We owe you our freedom," he said. "Without you and the others, we would have been overtaken."

The man glanced at Beran's hand. "You would have done the same, if you were able."

"I hope I would have the courage."

"It took no courage. I spent fourteen months in a Turkish galley. I had no wish to go back."

"How did you escape?"

"No one escapes from a galley. We were captured by the Venetians. My old captors took my place at the oars."

"It took determination to go back to sea after such an experience."

The other pilgrim shrugged. "I made a promise." He volunteered nothing more of his history, and though Beran wondered at the cause of his reluctance to take up a weapon against his old tormentors, he did not ask.

Whether their numbers discouraged attackers or luck was on their side, the band of pilgrims reached their goal unmolested. In the shadow of the walls of Jerusalem they saw a pitiful spectacle: those who had come this far and had no way of paying the final toll, a gold piece from each pilgrim. Hundreds of ragged, half-starved figures lay outside the walls. Too weak and dispirited to beg, they searched each group of new arrivals for a familiar face or some generous lord who would answer their supplications and gain them entry into the city. Beran felt their torment; for it must be torment indeed to come so close and then be barred. But having paid the toll, he was close to beggary himself and could offer no help.

In the weeks that followed, Beran visited the sites of pilgrimage. He saw the pillar of Pilate and witnessed a devout pilgrim having himself scourged before the spot, as Christ had been beaten. He knelt before the Holy Sepulcher, stood on Calvary, walked the narrow streets where every house and every corner had a heritage of sacred meaning. He prayed; he fasted; he wept bitterly, wrung with remorse for his youthful wickedness and folly; but all his prayers and penitence only left him convinced that he could never find forgiveness. Others confessed their sins, and immersed themselves in the waters of the Jordan, and were reborn in innocence. Not he. He dared not visit the holy river, fearful that his immersion would taint and blacken the waters with his sin. Repent as he might, Beran knew that he was beyond hope of mercy and unworthy even to beg for it.

He could never return to his wife and children, for his presence would be a sword over their heads. He resolved to remain here, wandering the desert in perpetual exile. Perhaps, in time, through some miracle, he would find mercy. If not, he would bring suffering on none but himself.

He traveled without aim, following roads to their end and striding on over trackless ground until he could see to go no farther, sleeping in the open more often than under shelter. He saw men and women the color of gold, and copper, and ebony, and heard languages he had never heard before. He moved freely among them all. He needed no language. His countenance spoke for him.

His frame became more gaunt than it had ever been during his early years of wandering. His hair was streaked with white, and his skin, where it was not burnished by wind and sun, was pallid and dry with age. And still he wandered, ever farther from his home.

With the passing of years, his mind and memory grew confused. He often wondered if the past life that he remembered had all been a dream from which he would one day awaken. It might be that he had never met the old man, never married, never been a juggler; that his family still lived and labored in the village below Sir Morier's castle, and that he himself was still a child, lost and confused in a troubling dream. It was possible, too, that all his memories, even the clear images of childhood, were a delusion; that he had always been here; that the filthy bandage on his right hand concealed a wound from some forgotten mishap in the desert, long ago. Perhaps he had been attacked by bandits and left dazed and injured in his mind as well as his body; he might even have been one of the attackers, abandoned by his accomplices. He no longer knew. He was certain only that he had done something wrong, and that he must suffer in atonement.

Once, when Beran was traveling with a caravan of traders, the old man appeared at the fireside late in the night. The guards were out of sight and hearing, and all the rest were asleep. Beran recognized the apparition as a figure from the past, but not a friend. The old man smiled in a pleasant manner and seated himself at Beran's side. Beran turned away and gazed into the fire. He did not want to speak to him.

"Why do you deceive yourself? No one denies me, ever. We have a bargain," he said to Beran.

"Do you pursue me?"

"You flatter yourself. I merely stop for a moment in passing, to prod your memory. I must be about my business and my pleasure. Oh, I delight in observing the things you do to one another, and hearing the excuses you make for them. One can learn much from lesser beings."

"And what is your business?"

"It is quite beyond your understanding. I have many agreements such as yours—more than you can imagine."

"We have no agreement," Beran said. "It's all a dream. You are a dream."

The old man pointed a finger in admonition. "It would be well for you to fulfill your bargain without delay, before you can do so no longer."

"What is our bargain? Who are you?"

"Don't pretend. You know."

"No. I reject you. I deny you."

Beran rubbed his eyes, and the old man was gone. Everyone around him slept, and the desert was silent. He sat by the fire deep in thought for a long time. He had not slept; it had not been a dream; yet it could not have been real. He had to face the fearful truth that he had indeed lost his reason, and now saw and heard things that were not there. At last he drifted off into sleep and dreamed a troubling dream.

He was on a gloomy plain in some far land where all was barren and bleak. The few trees he saw were twisted naked things with splintered limbs. The sky was dark, but he saw clearly. A procession passed before him on a broad highway. Crowned kings and nobles rode slowly by on richly caparisoned steeds, beggars on crutches hobbled and limped by their side, and behind them stretched an endless train of ladies in elegant litters, ragged peasants, mitred bishops with croziers in hand, knights in armor, tavern revelers, friars, soldiers with limbs missing and bloodless wounds gaping in their heads and bodies. Beran sensed the opulence of the well-born, the sheen of their silks and glitter of jewels, though under this sullen sky all was gray and dull to the eye. He noticed for the first time that the air was filled with fine ash, slowly falling on the gray land, mantling all in its drabness. He saw familiar figures, too: Sejourne and the mutilated juggler and the dancing lady, the dead soldiers in Sir Morier's castle, the thief he had slain. All were pale and hollow-eyed, and walked in silence. Then he was among them, one of them, and the ashen air was filled with their moaning and weeping. Crawling things scuttled among them and over them. All around, appearing and vanishing and reappearing, were a legion of stunted demons, humped, misshapen black things with eyes and tongues of yellow flame, horns jutting from their ears, and voices like grating metal. They jeered and taunted the pallid figures, breathed sulphurous, stinking breath into their faces, and jabbed them cruelly with fiery spears, gibbering and laughing all the while, and the crawling things squirmed into the fresh wounds. The procession traveled on, passive under the abuse and suffering, too deep in despair to react to bodily pain, too hopeless even to groan or cry out, and Beran, no longer of their number, watched from a great distance.

These were the damned, being led off to their place of eternal suffering. They had died unrepentant. He was repentant now, but too late, far too late. He had long concealed his wickedness, lived with it as a daily secret, masked it with an outward show. He could not hope to be forgiven. He would suffer a worse fate than this.

The next day, he overheard two of the traders speaking of a hermit who lived in the desert somewhere near. He was a friar who had come on pilgrimage and stayed in the waste places of the Holy Land to lead a life of prayer and penitence. The traders spoke of the man lightly, dismissing him as a fool or a lunatic. To Beran, their idle banter was a revelation.

Coming so quickly after the old man's visit and the dream, their words could only be a message meant for him. He must find the hermit. Since coming to the Holy Land he had fled the presence of those who, he believed, could not begin to understand his plight and would only judge and reject him, or offer empty words of consolation or advice. But he had no more desire to flee, only an overwhelming need to unburden himself to someone who would listen and, though he would not forgive, would not condemn. While his senses remained, and his mind still had some grip on reality, he had to act.

He begged the traders for more information. They were decent men, and his sincerity touched them. They told him what little they knew, pointed out the way, and provided him with food and water. He set out alone into the desert.

He found the hermit with his last strength. On his hands and knees, his food and water gone, too weak to stand, he crawled to within sight of the holy man's dwelling, and there collapsed, calling out for his help. The hermit found him, carried him back to his crude stone shelter, and nursed him. When he revived, though he was still painfully weak, Beran threw himself at the hermit's feet and poured out his story.

The holy man listened without interrupting, and showed no surprise. When Beran had told all, he said only, "Your sins are forgiven. Stay, and heal."

Beran dragged himself back to his hard bed and slept more soundly than he had since leaving home. In the morning, when the holy man had prayed, they talked. Beran sat and listened like a child.

"You spoke as though you were lost, but while a man lives, his soul is his own. We must never despair," said the hermit.

"How could I hope for mercy?"

"There is always hope of mercy."

"But I bargained my soul away. I was the worst of sinners."

The hermit smiled and laid a reassuring hand on Beran's head. "You are too ambitious. You wanted to be the greatest juggler in the world, and your ambition caused you great suffering. You came to believe that you were the greatest sinner, and that, too, has caused you suffering. You are a man, Beran, with all a man's strengths and weaknesses. You bargained with the Father of Lies. He deceived you, and under his influence you long deceived yourself."

"But I saw. . . . He gave life to my wooden hand."

"Unbind the hand."

Beran tugged at the cloth, which was so frayed and tattered that it fell away easily. The flesh at the socket was red and inflamed, and the wooden hand itself locked into a tight fist. The hermit reached out and moved the stiff fingers, one by one, until they were spread wide.

"Move your fingers," he said.

Beran strained, and the fingers did not move. The hand was a lifeless artifact of wood. "But it moved. I juggled with this hand just as I did with my own hand."

"Who saw you juggle but yourself and the old man?"

"No one."

"And you concealed the restoration of your hand from your wife and children, did you not?"

Beran nodded, confused, only beginning to grasp the extent of the old man's deception and his own willingness to be deceived. He still did not understand. He had seen the wooden hand work with all the dexterity of flesh and blood, felt the fingers and sinews moving. And now he knew that the hand had never lived, never moved except when he manipulated the wooden joints with his good hand. It was no more than a clever piece of workmanship, as it always had been.

"He cannot give life to a thing carved of wood. He is the enemy of life. He does not restore, he only destroys," the holy man went on.

"Am I truly free?"

"You were free of him when you first repented the bargain, but he battened on your weakness and your fear. He always comes to us in our times of fear and weakness and shame. Our despair is his strength, and you surrendered to despair. Run from him no more. Return to your wife and daughter."

"What will I do when he comes for me? I cannot face him alone. He frightens me, and I am unable to resist."

"You will not be alone. Have hope and faith, and you will be prepared to face him. Believe that, and return to your home."

"But when he comes . . . ?"

"He comes to me often, to tempt me with riches, luxuries, fair women; all the things the world offers. Confront him and reject him. As long as you reject him, you remain free."

"He is so powerful. . . ."

"He is powerful indeed. We must never forget that.

He is a fallen angel; though fallen, still an angel; an angel, though fallen. However tainted, his is an angelic nature, as far above our human nature as we are above a dog's. But there is One more powerful. Always remember that."

12

The
Reckoning

The inn was run by a handsome matron and her husband. At first Beran did not recognize Marie-Jeanne, but the sight of her own daughter, so like the little girl he remembered seeing at her mother's inn those many years ago, made it clear to him that she was now the mistress here, and a child no longer.

He entered as a palmer seeking food and rest. He kept the stump of his hand concealed under his cloak and his face in shadow, but there was little danger of his being recognized. Time and hardship had taken their toll. He was slightly stooped, and walked slowly with measured steps, like a man who has come far and knows that he may yet have far to go. His cheeks were hollow, his hand and face darkened by a sun unimagined in this land where the skies were often gray and gloomy. His hair was heavily streaked with white, and he had a short white beard, roughly trimmed. He weighed far less than he had weighed when last he sat at a table in this room.

No other guests were at the inn this night. The innkeeper was a young man, fresh-faced and friendly. Beran had a vague memory of having seen him before, but could not recall his name. The innkeeper greeted Beran and, when he ate, sat at table with him and exchanged news. Beran's garments were well worn, and he appeared to be a man with some tales to tell, if he so chose. They talked for a time, the innkeeper of the city and Beran of the world beyond, and as they finished a second mug of ale, Beran asked if the inn had not once been owned by a man with a wooden hand.

"It was indeed, but that was long ago. My wife is that man's daughter, and she was scarcely more than a child when he left."

Beran gave a start. It was not Marie-Jeanne he had seen—it was his younger daughter, Annette. He should have realized. The innkeeper seemed not to notice his surprise, and Beran asked, "Why did he leave?"

"He had the call to go on pilgrimage. It came suddenly, and he obeyed. He was prosperous and well liked, but he left everything without hesitation." The innkeeper leaned closer and said in a lowered, confiding voice, "There's those who say he was fleeing some old enemy, but I don't believe it. No guilty man could have had such fine daughters, or won the love of a woman like his wife."

Beran swallowed a sip of ale. Looking down at the tabletop, he asked, "Does anyone know what became of him?"

The innkeeper shrugged. "No one has heard a word since the day he left. His wife asked everyone who might have known, but no one could tell her."

Beran felt a chill of apprehension to hear Anna referred to in such a way. "What's become of his wife?"

"She managed the inn by herself for as long as she could, and her daughters helped her when they were old enough. I worked for her. The older daughter married a farmer and moved away, out on the forest road. They have a fine home. I married the younger daughter two years ago last harvest time, and we've been running the place since then."

"And the mother . . . ?"

"She's never stopped thinking of her husband. She's a sick woman now. The priest says it will be a miracle if she lives to see another spring."

"But she lives?"

The young man nodded, and Beran, rising, said, "May I see her? I think . . . I may be able to give her good news."

"About her husband?"

"Yes."

"Is he alive?" The joy in the young man's face and

voice were unfeigned. "Bless you, stranger. If you bring any news of him, we're all beholden to you."

"He is alive, and will return."

"This will make her well. She's been bad for the past week, but news of her husband will be a tonic. Come this way."

He led Beran up a familiar flight of stairs, to the very room where he had once confronted the old man. "She seldom leaves the room now, not since the last sickness. It's difficult for her to walk."

He tapped softly at the door and, when he heard no response, tapped once again. After a short time he pushed the door open. Anna lay in the bed—their bed—and the innkeeper said, "A visitor. He brings news."

At the sight of his wife, pale and graying, lying still and shrunken under the heavy comforter, Beran could not hold back his tears. He hung back as the young man left, and as soon as they were alone, he fell on his knees at the bedside and said, "Anna, I've come home. I'll never leave you again. I went away to save you and the children, and to save myself, and I wronged us all."

She opened her eyes at the sound of his voice, and with a soft cry she reached out to take him in her arms in a feeble but fervent embrace. For a long time they did not speak. When she lay back, still holding his hand, she said slowly, "I knew you'd return. You said that one day you'd explain."

"I will. And I beg you to forgive me."

Shaking her head, smiling, she reached up to silence him with a touch on his lips. "You did what you believed was right. There is no question of forgiveness. Only tell me, tell me all."

Seating himself on the bed, he told her of his youthful ambition, and his impatience, and finally his reckless bargain. She drew a sudden breath and crossed herself, but said nothing. He went on, "He came to me and promised me my desire in return for my soul. He looked like a ragged old tinker. I told myself he was just a conjurer, but I knew."

"He was the old man . . . when you were so sick."

The juggler nodded. "I rejected him once, but the second time he came, I was alone and frightened. I accepted his offer. As a pledge of my faith, I offered him my right hand."

"Oh, my poor Beran," she murmured.

"I repented of the bargain and took to wandering, thinking to hide myself from him. I came to the court of Count Osostro. He cut off my right hand . . . but then, a few days later . . . he gave me gold and the letter that enabled us to save the inn. And I think the old man took his revenge on the count."

"Men say that the count was a wicked man."

"He was cruel and capricious, but he did me a good service. He died a terrible death, and I think it was because of me."

"They say he died as he deserved."

"Perhaps he did. But if I had spoken up, he might not have cut off my hand. I feared that I had condemned him by my silence. When the old man came to me—in this very room—I was so confused, so full of shame and guilt, that I was easy prey. He worked on my weakness, and I believed he had brought my hand back to life. I wanted to believe it. Then he tried to make me betray you and our daughters. He said that I need not give him my soul, but one of yours. I knew that I must leave, for your sakes."

"You could never have betrayed us."

"I might have. I'm a weak man, Anna. I feared my own weakness."

"But now you've returned."

"I'm ready to accept what must be."

His cloak had fallen aside as they spoke, and she saw the stump of his right arm. He caught her look of pain and pity, and before she could speak, he said, "I wandered for a long time in the desert before I found a holy man who helped me see the truth. In my wanderings, the arm became infected. I very nearly died on my way back to Jerusalem. Travelers found me in the desert, raving mad with the poison in my body. The monks had to cut away the rotten flesh to save my life. I stayed long in the hospital at Jerusalem. I might have been there still but for the kindness of an old friend, an honest knight who remembered me from long ago. He was very generous to me."

She struggled upright. "It was the old man's evil that poisoned your body and nearly captured your soul. Now that the hand is gone, he cannot take you. We're safe, Beran."

Beran held her close until her breathing became regular, and she slept. He laid her back on her pillow, clumsily but with loving gentleness, and drew the bedclothes around her. He was home, to stay with her and help her. Anna's assurance was comforting to hear, but he knew that his enemy was persistent. They were not safe. The greatest struggles lay ahead.

He turned from the bed and saw the old man sitting on a stool by the fireplace, looking at him. He felt a stab of fear. He was not surprised by the old man's appearance, only by its coming so quickly. He had hoped he would have time to gather strength and prepare himself.

"So, you have returned. And your allotted time is growing short," the old man said.

"It is not for you to measure my life span."

"How fierce we are. How bold and defiant," said the old man, smiling as an adult might smile at the bravado of a child in the dark.

"You have no hold on me, no power over me but what I give you, and I give you none. I renounced you long ago. I rejected you, and I reject you now," Beran said. His voice trembled as he spoke, but he did not hesitate.

"Of the fifty years I promised you, more than half are gone. How brave will you be on the last day, when it's time to fulfill your part of the bargain? I've been generous to you—more than generous."

"Generous with lies and deceit."

The old man shook his head sadly. "Such ingratitude. You have fallen among my enemies, and they've filled your head with doubt. But you know that you were the greatest of all jugglers, the greatest ever, in all the world. You know that the wooden hand came to life and did your bidding as if it were flesh and blood. You cannot doubt those things. And you cannot doubt that you are in thrall to me and can never break your thralldom."

"While I live, you do not own my soul."

"And will you live forever?" the old man asked. Raising open hands in a gentle gesture, he said, "But I have not asked for your soul. Have you forgotten? I released you from that obligation. And I will be even more generous. I will no longer require an innocent soul in place of yours. No, I demand only a single soul, any one at all, old or young, innocent or wicked, in exchange for the one you owe me. Bring me that, and you're free."

"Your generosity is as deceitful as your gifts. You

know that if I damn another to save myself, I damn myself as well."

"Your wanderings have sharpened your mind. You have become a theologian. But tell me, wise man, what of those already hurrying on their way to me? Thousands come to me each day. If you speed one more on the way, what blame can attach to you? You need not go far to find them. They are everywhere. This innkeeper, for instance, Richard, who is married to your daughter."

"He is a decent man. He was concerned for my wife."

"Oh, a charming fellow to travelers, but greedy and a coward. He is indeed much concerned for your wife. He is eager to own this inn, and the sight of your wife lying helpless in her room puts thoughts in his head. One night—if only he can muster the courage—he will slip into her room and place a pillow over her face. Oh, yes, he will, I know he will. It will be a matter of moments, and then—"

"He showed nothing but admiration for her. He will resist you," Beran said.

"We shall see. There is also your stepdaughter. You remember Marie-Jeanne as a pretty child. She has grown into a lovely woman, but an unhappy one, married to a dull brute, a drunken lecher who beats her and torments their children. Every night she dreams of plunging a knife in his heart as he lies snoring at her side. She has seen him fondling the servant girl, and she fears for their daughter, but she dares not speak. One day she will kill him. All I ask of you—"

"Stop! Stop this foul talk!" Beran cried.

In the same subdued, reasonable tone, the old man went on. "And what of your wife? Oh, she is shriven now, and ready for death. Sickness makes you all so very pious, but what of those years when you were far away and she longed to have a man in her bed? Do you think she denied herself? She was a fine woman, and every man who came to the inn looked at her with hunger in his heart. Do you believe she rejected them all?"

"Yes."

The old man laughed softly, like a faint rustling in the forest. "Are you such an expert on chastity?"

"I know that Anna loves me as I love her."

"Remember your own youth, Beran. Remember the girls in the alehouses and inns, and the servants at the castles and manor houses, and the wives and daughters who were bedazzled by your skill and gave themselves to you so willingly. Is your Anna better than they? Have you any right or reason to expect—"

"Go! You lie, you can do nothing but lie, and I reject you utterly. I pray—"

The old man gave a cry that turned to a snarl and then to an unearthly rasping shriek. He burst open like a pod of corruption, swelling and splitting and tearing free from his human bounds to reveal himself in his true essence. His form became something unhuman and horrible, and other things, loathly things, erupted from his flesh to crawl upon him, and scuttle beneath him, and buzz about him. The room expanded into a dizzying infinite space, and Beran was adrift in a cosmos of icy darkness that seared his flesh and lungs with a cold that burned hotter than flame. The air was empty of substance, and his lungs struggled helplessly against the vacuum; yet that same air was thick with foul stench and imbecile gibbering and the tangible shrieking of the hopeless damned like spikes driven into his brain, while the crawling and flying things tore at his body, peeling and shredding flesh and sinew, gnawing at raw bone. Gagging and gasping, he struggled to turn away. He buried his face in his cloak, thrusting out his bandaged arm before him to ward off the horror, but his cloak was whirled away in the blast, his reluctant eyelids were torn open, and he saw.

A coil of fire erupted from the monstrous apparition and clung to the stump of Beran's arm. At its touch an appendage of flame appeared, many-fingered, joined to his flesh but alive with a will of its own. It reached out to claw at him. Beran opened his mouth to scream, and the thick sulphurous air filled his mouth and lungs, choking and gagging him until his stomach revolted. The crawling and flying things swarmed over him, invading ears and mouth and nostrils, tearing at his flesh and crunching his bones with the sound of shears and grindstones.

He crumpled to his knees, but there was no surface beneath him and he fell flailing and clutching out at the emptiness. In pain and terror he shrieked out a desperate prayer.

At the utterance, his hellish surroundings vanished. He was once again within the four familiar walls of his own bedroom. He lay huddled on the floor before the fireplace, the bitterness of his own vomit in his mouth. The stool was overturned. The little room was otherwise as it had been, unchanged but for a faint foul odor that quickly dissipated.

The monstrous hand was gone. The stump of Beran's arm throbbed, for he had struck it in falling, but it was otherwise scatheless, the skin unbroken and unburned. His body was whole, and free of wounds. All the horror had been one last deception. His heart was pounding, and he was soaked in sweat and breathless, but he felt the freedom and peace a man feels upon awakening from a long fever, and he savored the moment even though he knew that this might be only the first of many trials.

Anna lay pale and unmoving on the bed. A sudden panic seized him at the thought that the old man had vented his rage on her. But when he knelt at her side and took her hand, she sighed and opened her eyes. At a glance into his pale face and glittering eyes she knew, and clutched his hand hard.

"He was here. But now he's gone," she whispered.

"But you—"

"Now I will recover." She smiled at him and closed her eyes.

Soon after that day, Anna began to regain strength. At the end of a month, she and Beran left the inn in the hands of Annette and Richard and moved back to the cottage by the river where they had lived when they first arrived.

The old man's onslaughts did not cease. His struggle with Beran could end only at the moment of death. He came again many times, in many guises. Sometimes he courted Beran like a lover, with gentle blandishments, and sometimes he leered at him silently from within the face of a speaker. At times he merely flickered into sight for an instant at a turn in the stair, or in a doorway, and immediately vanished; at other times he attacked like a famished beast. Beran's resistance never slackened.

His remaining years were in many ways placid and happy. The old man's tales of Marie-Jeanne's brutal marriage, of Richard's greed and Anna's infidelity, all turned out to be as false as his threats and promises. Both daughters were happily married to good and loving men, and Anna's devotion to her husband's memory, and her unshakable faith in his return, had made her almost a legend here in the city and elsewhere, as travelers had told of her steadfastness.

Beran's homecoming was a great event, celebrated with prayer and feasting. He made an offering of thanks at the church, where his scrip and bourdonnée were mounted over a side altar for all to see. He had been known to nearly everyone in the city, and well liked, and now he had new tales to tell them. Old friends and acquaintances, and those who knew him only by name, were eager to hear the account of his travels. He was saddened to learn that Bruno had died in his absence, but he consoled himself with the knowledge that Bruno's works survived and would outlast the city itself. And, too, the new master of the workshop, one of Bruno's assistants, was an old friend and frequent visitor to the inn. One link with his good memories had been broken, but a new one was forged.

The city had grown during his absence, and many things had changed. Nowadays the council were often called upon to decide questions for which they had no precedent. New problems of justice and the common defense, of commerce and industry and provisioning, seemed to confront them almost monthly. Unprepared for such challenges, they were often baffled and divided. They felt the need for someone with experience of other lands and their ways, a widely traveled man whom they could trust to aid them in their deliberations. Beran was asked again and again to advise the councilors, which he gladly did, and at last requested to take a place among them. He declined the honor, saying that his experience and wisdom—such as they were—would always be at the service of the council, but such strength as remained to him was needed for the care of his wife.

Anna never recovered fully, but she lived long enough to see the birth of three more grandchildren, and her death, when it came, was serene. The old enemy chose the occasion of her last sickness to make his most prolonged and violent onslaught. Beran resisted, but the effort broke his strength. He survived Anna for less than a year, only long enough to see their oldest grandchild married.

To the very end of his life, he went three times each week to the church, where he prayed for his wife, and for the count Osostro, and for all his other benefactors.

IMAGINING
BERAN'S
WORLD

he setting of *The Juggler* is a real time and place, and I've tried to portray its life and spirit accurately. Beran and the rest of the people in the story are completely fictional. But as in any book set in a different time and place, there is some historical reality in the imaginary characters, and some fiction in the portrayal of the real world.

Beran's world was very different from ours. We would find it monotonous and isolated and very confining. Most people never ventured more than a few miles from home in their entire lives, and had no wish to do otherwise. Strangers were generally treated with suspicion, and sometimes with outright hostility.

The people of the Middle Ages were just as intelligent and talented as we are. They built cities and institutions that have lasted until our time, created great works of art, and made discoveries that are the foundations of the modern world. But they saw life through very different eyes. To them, hell and the devil were real and tangible. Evil might be lurking anywhere around them, in any form. Any unusual occurrence—a storm, an eclipse or meteor, an outbreak of illness—might be an omen or portent of disaster. Pilgrimage offered hope of escaping evil and saving one's soul.

Individual people had different motives, just as they do today. Some went on a pilgrimage or a Crusade out of deep piety and religious belief. Some went out of fear of hell, and some went simply because it was a chance to travel and enjoy new experiences.

This is the historical world I hoped to present in *The Juggler*. Information about the great events and institutions of the Middle Ages—the plagues, the Crusades, feudalism, knighthood, pilgrimage, and the Church—is not hard to find. We know a great deal about how people worked and ate and dressed. We know how life was lived in castle, city, and village, what travel was like, and how someone set about going on pilgrimage. The higher people ranked on the social scale, the more information we have about them. We know less about how ordinary people really felt and thought and reacted and lived their daily lives. And we know very little about jugglers.

Jugglers were not considered important or respectable people in the Middle Ages, and few people bothered to write about them except to condemn them. Little more was written about the people who might have gathered together at a fair, or on a market day, to watch entertainers like Beran and his companions. How a medieval peasant mother and father spoke to their children, what serfs talked about on their way to work, and how a juggler actually went about learning to be a juggler, didn't interest serious people. The serious people were concerned with wars and plagues, kings and queens, saints and explorers and philosophers.

I drew my information about village and castle life and people from *Life in Medieval England*, by J. J. Bagley; *Scenes and Characters of the Middle Ages*, by Edward Lewes Cutts; and *The Knight in History*, by Frances Gies. Frances and Joseph Gies have written other books about aspects of medieval life, and they are all very good.

The Galleys at Lepanto, by Jack Beeching, was the chief source of information about conditions on the galleys. It's a fine piece of historical writing, as exciting as any adventure novel. *Sailing Ships in Words and Pictures*, by Bjorn Landström, and *Ships*, by Enzo Angelucci and Attilio Cucari, were full of helpful illustrations. *Pilgrimage*, by Jonathan Sumption, contains complete information about the great age of pilgrimage and the customs and traditions and dangers connected with it. It was very helpful. For the life of jugglers and traveling entertainers, I drew on *English Wayfaring Life in the Middle Ages*, by J. J. Jusserand, and *The Medieval Underworld*, by Andrew McCall.

Scholarly and historical books gave me the details of life. Beran's bargain with the old man is drawn from legend. The belief that one can make a deal with the devil is a very old one (Christopher Marlowe wrote about it in *Doctor Faustus* over four hundred years ago), and it still turns up in books, films, and even musical comedies. Our times are a long way from the Middle Ages, but some things do not change, even over centuries. There will always be people willing to bargain with evil—with the devil himself, if necessary—in order to achieve their desire.

To learn how people in Beran's world might have spoken and acted, I looked to literature. Ben Jonson's *Volpone*, Chaucer's *Canterbury Tales*, and *The Vision of Piers Plowman*, by William Langland, gave me an idea of how people might have behaved at taverns, fairs, and inns. Herman Hesse's *Narcissus and Goldmund* provided suggestions of what a medieval craftsman's workshop might have been like. Other details came from memory. The works of Master Bruno, for example, are based on items I've seen in museums. He is imaginary, but his works are real.

I read other books, of course, but these were the

most helpful. I'm sure that many others things now forgotten—books I've read, and objects I've seen— have left their impression in my memory and turned up in this book. I wish I could give all of them the credit they deserve.